"Wha...

Diana and Adam stared at each other as his words echoed around them. Diana wished the floor would open and swallow her. Of all the men she could have worked for, why did it have to be him?

His glittering brown eyes raked her from head to toe, taking in her pale face and severe hair-style, her serviceable dress and her sensible shoes.

"Don't tell me you're the new housekeeper?" he questioned incredulously.

"Temporarily only."

"You can say that again! I was told you were a *cordon bleu* chef. I wasn't aware that they did a course in burnt offerings!"

Angered by the heavy sarcasm, she did her best not to let it show. "That was a long time ago— I've learned a lot since then."

"I hope so. You had a lot *to* learn."

ROBERTA LEIGH wrote her first book at the age of nineteen and since then has written more than seventy romance novels, as well as many books and film series for children. She has also been an editor of a woman's magazine and produced a teen magazine, but writing romance fiction remains one of her greatest joys. She lives in Hampstead, London, and has one son.

Books by Roberta Leigh

ROBERTA LEIGH

Not His Kind of Woman

Harlequin Books

TORONTO • NEW YORK • LONDON
AMSTERDAM • PARIS • SYDNEY • HAMBURG
STOCKHOLM • ATHENS • TOKYO • MILAN
MADRID • WARSAW • BUDAPEST • AUCKLAND

Harlequin Presents first edition September 1993
ISBN 0-373-11585-7

Original hardcover edition published in 1992
by Mills & Boon Limited

NOT HIS KIND OF WOMAN

CHAPTER ONE

LOOKING round the crowded terrace, filled with 'beautiful people' whose predictable gossip bored her to tears, Diana Farrow suddenly decided she was sick to death of the whole scene.

Setting down her wine glass, she ran through the house to where her red Mercedes convertible was parked among the Maseratis and Porsches in the forecourt of the Georgian mansion.

'I must have been mad to come here!' she muttered as she shot down the driveway, silky blonde curls blowing in the breeze. 'If I don't find an interesting job soon, I'll die of boredom.'

Trouble was, she hadn't trained for anything useful, and since leaving finishing school had spent most of her time enjoying herself. Poor little rich girl, she reflected moodily, and would happily have changed places with anyone who had the talent to do something creative.

The last time she had worked hard—the few hours a week she put in at a Knightsbridge florist was hardly taxing, either mentally or physically—had been for her A levels. Yet whenever she suggested training for a profession, or going to secretarial college, her mother always voiced the same objection.

'I'm much happier if I know you're around when I need you. You're such a comfort to me when I get my depressions.'

Someone with a stronger motivation to work would have rebutted this, but knowing how severe her mother's depressions could be made it difficult for Diana to stand her ground. Yet this did not mitigate her frustration at her aimless existence, and when she drew up outside her parents' Knightsbridge home and found she didn't have the key to the front door, she felt like kicking it. Blast! They were out for the day, and so were the staff.

Having left most of her friends at the party—and in her present mood she didn't feel like seeing any of the others—she debated what to do. Suddenly remembering she had heard there was an interesting exhibition at the Tate, she decided it was as good a place as any to while away time. Besides, she hadn't been to a gallery or a concert for at least a year. What a Philistine she was!

Standing in the queue, she was oblivious of how she stood out in the crowd, despite being a pint-sized five feet two. Corn-gold hair curled around a delicately featured face, slender body was skimmed by a red and white Valentino dress that gently outlined breasts and hips, while the short skirt and matching high-heeled sandals emphasised shapely legs.

There was a flurry ahead, and she soon found herself inside the gallery, surrounded by vast canvases of Pop art, which she loathed. She'd have enjoyed herself more at the zoo!

'I wish I knew what it meant,' a well-groomed elderly woman commented, frowning at a montage of bottle-tops and labels.

'An advert for refuse,' Diana replied. 'To me, it's a load of junk.'

'Junk?' a deep male voice questioned on her other side, and Diana swung round on the speaker: a young man in his mid-twenties, with unruly black hair, a pugnacious jaw and athletic build.

'Junk,' she asserted.

'Why?' he asked, the quirk of his thick eyebrows giving him a sardonic look.

'Because it's meaningless.'

'On the contrary. Pop art reflects the basic elements of today's culture.'

'I hardly think that qualifies it as art.'

'Art doesn't have to be beautiful. Life can be ugly, and art should reflect it, should make people aware of what's going on around them.'

Diana watched him as he spoke, seeing intelligence in the dark brown eyes, and obstinacy in the firm nose and chin, though it was mitigated by a well-shaped mouth that had a markedly humorous curve to it. Struck by his looks, she was less so by his argument, though as they continued round the gallery and she listened to his comments, she began seeing the canvases with new eyes.

'How come you're so knowledgeable?' she enquired.

'Because I read and look.'

'Are you in the art world?'

'Exactly the opposite,' he smiled, showing strong white teeth. 'I'm studying electronics.'

'How interesting,' Diana lied, having only a vague idea what it entailed.

'I'm going for a coffee,' he stated, turning away.

'Me too,' she said, curious to find out more about him. 'We can see the rest of the exhibition afterwards.'

'You've seen the best. The others are just fillers.'

'You've seen this exhibition before, then?'

'The Tate is one of my regular Sunday haunts. You'll probably like the Gauguin exhibition better. It starts next week. Plenty of exotic colour, and if you know something about the artist, easy to understand.'

She was relieved to hear a familiar name. 'I adore his Tahitian women,' she said, hoping to impress with her knowledge.

Without replying he preceded her to the coffee-shop in the basement. Taking a tray each, they waited their turn at the self-service counter. Diana discovered she was hungry and helped herself to a packet of smoked salmon sandwiches, a chocolate éclair, and coffee. He settled for coffee only.

'If that's all you're having we didn't need two trays,' Diana smiled at him, and he smiled back as she walked past the cashier.

'That'll be five pounds, please,' the girl called to her.

Diana looked over her shoulder, but the young man made no move to pay, and flustered, she set down her tray and opened her purse.

What a boor to behave so badly over such a trifling amount, she thought irritably, and marched over to a table at the far side of the room. He hadn't struck her as ill-mannered, though she had been surprised to learn he was a student. At his age he should have qualified, not still be at university. Perhaps he had taken time off to see the world first, as many of her friends had.

Resolutely she refused to glance at him, but was aware of him taking a chair at a table some distance away. He was very attractive, even in well-worn denims and washed out sweater. The thin wool clung to his broad shoulders and the pushed-up sleeves revealed lean strong arms, the muscles bulging.

Hurriedly she ate her sandwich and éclair, gulped down her coffee, and rose. She walked past him without a glance, and her heart thumped as his chair scraped back and he started walking alongside her.

'Enjoy the Gauguin—if you come,' he said.

'I'm not sure if I can find the time,' she answered sweetly.

They reached the foyer, and without a backward glance he sauntered out, leaving Diana surprised and angry; she was not used to being brushed off—usually it was the other way around.

Unwilling to leave in case he thought she was chasing after him, she wandered around until she found herself in front of Rodin's *The Kiss*. Her eyes ranged over the

NOT HIS KIND OF WOMAN

curves and hollows of the two bodies clinging together, and she felt strangely disturbed as, inexplicably, she envisaged herself in the arms of the man she had just met.

Berating herself for being a fool, she headed for her car. He meant nothing to her. She knew a dozen men more attractive, and given the chance they would fall over themselves to take her out.

CHAPTER TWO

As DIANA lounged on her bed the following evening, she wondered what was happening to her. She had always found shopping exhilarating, yet this afternoon she had been impatient to get out of Harvey Nichols, where her mother had taken her to buy some summer dresses. Unexpectedly her thoughts turned to the Tate and the young man she had met there...

If she knew where to contact him she'd ask him to be her escort at her best friend's nineteenth birthday party. He was so macho, all the other girls there would drool with envy! She pulled a face, knowing it was stupid to consider running after someone who hadn't even wanted to pay for a snack! She thought of the men she knew—most of whom bored her silly—and admitted how marvellous it would be if she met the love of her life at Jane's party on Saturday.

Unfortunately she didn't, though within minutes of arriving there she was surrounded by her usual entourage of young men, all eager to please, all equally dull.

Dawn was streaking the sky when she finally returned home, and it was midday Sunday before the barking of dogs in the street awoke her. Staggering out of bed, she drew aside the drapes. It was a grey, rainy day, definitely not suitable for tennis, which she had planned. But what to do instead? The word 'Gauguin' flashed into her mind, bringing with it a picture not of the artist, but the fresh-skinned, aquiline-nosed young man who had been irritatingly in her thoughts this past week.

10

Slipping into a housecoat, she hurried downstairs to make sure the exhibition was definitely at the Tate.

'Why the sudden interest in art?' Her father lowered the business section of the *Sunday Times* and peered at her over his glasses as she scanned the arts section.

'You should be pleased I'm trying to improve myself,' Diana grinned, unwilling to tell him the real reason. Planting a kiss on his cheek, she dashed upstairs to dress.

Arriving at the Tate, she was disappointed to see no sign of the man she had come to find, and dejectedly strolled through the gallery, barely noticing the paintings.

Her despondency stayed with her until, reaching a smaller room, she spotted him, hands plunged into his pockets, totally absorbed in a painting of a young girl. A quick glance at the catalogue told her it was *Girl with Mango*, on loan from the Cone Collection in Baltimore.

'That's certainly not junk,' she murmured, coming to stand beside him.

He turned and smiled, not appearing in the least surprised to see her. 'The public rubbished it when it was first seen. They did the same to all the other Impressionists too. They were the Pop artists of their day.'

'But they weren't difficult to understand,' she argued. 'Not like that bottle-top painting.'

'In their day they were just as incomprehensible. People were accustomed to the lifelike exactness of Hals, Rembrandt, Rubens, and when they were faced with brightly coloured canvases, and images which didn't come into focus until you stood way back from them, they threw up their hands in horror.'

'You really do know a lot about art,' she said naïvely.

'Compared with whom?' he smiled.

'Me—for a start!'

He shrugged. 'If you're interested, it's easy to learn.'

'How about teaching me? You could start right now!'

'I don't have the time. I have to go.'

He walked away and Diana watched him, mouth gaping. He couldn't leave her. Not now when she had found him! Impulsively she ran after him.

'I have a couple of tickets for a concert at the Festival Hall next Thursday,' she lied. 'My girlfriend can't make it, and I'd be awfully pleased if you came instead.'

'What's the programme?'

Piqued that he had not accepted the offer without questioning, she almost told him to forget it.

'Beethoven,' she stated. If it wasn't, she could always say she had muddled the dates.

'I'll be happy to come with you,' he said.

'Good. I'll meet you there at seven-fifteen. My name's Diana Farrow, by the way.'

'Mine's Adam Brooke,' he reciprocated, and with a laconic nod went off.

She seethed. It wouldn't have hurt him to have chatted a bit longer, and not leave her standing like a lemon. 'I must be mad,' she muttered, wishing she hadn't run after him. Supposing all the tickets were sold? She didn't even know where to contact him!

But luck was on her side: seats were still available, and it *was* a Beethoven concert. She bought the best they had and determined to go to the library to read up on the music they were going to hear. She might not know enough about art to have an intelligent discussion, but she'd pin Adam's ears back with her knowledge of Mr B!

A rush of orders at the florist where she worked—she had taken the job in a fit of boredom—gave her little chance to find out about the composer, and it wasn't until Wednesday that she managed to get to the library.

Instant knowledge on Beethoven proved difficult, for there was enough written about him to keep her busy for a lifetime, and rather than make a fool of herself trying to impress with a little knowledge, she abandoned the project and rang her friend to ask if she wanted to browse around the shops. Jane, a curvaceous, curly-haired brunette who worked part-time in her brother's estate agency, was happy to accept.

'Hugo just said I could leave early, and I was wondering how to fill in a few hours. Can you pick me up?'

Half an hour later they were driving round Sloane Square in search of a parking place.

'You've hardly any petrol,' Jane warned her.

Diana glanced at the gauge and frowned. 'Is there a garage nearby?'

'Take the first left, and then right. There's one on the corner.'

Relieved, Diana did as she was told, but as she reached the forecourt the engine died.

'Wait here,' she told Jane. 'I'll see if I can find someone to push the car to the pump.'

A few yards away a uniformed attendant was bent over the open bonnet of a van, and she hurried over to him.

'Excuse me, but could you help me? I've run out of petrol.'

The man straightened and turned towards her. Stunned, she found herself looking into chestnut-brown eyes set into a high-cheekboned face, marred by a streak of grease down one side. It was Adam Brooke!

'H-hello,' she stammered.

'Fancy seeing you here,' he grinned. 'How did you find me?'

'By accident, not design,' she said quickly, hoping Jane hadn't heard. Some hope! Her friend had the car window open and was listening to every word. 'I—er—my car's run out of petrol,' she repeated.

'Not to worry. You steer and I'll push.'

Avoiding his eyes, Diana returned to the car and got behind the wheel. Adam moved to the rear and placed both hands on the boot. The car rolled smoothly forward, and as it came alongside the pump, Diana put on the brake, then glanced into the driving-mirror to see Adam filling the petrol tank.

'Do you two know each other?' Jane asked, as Adam straightened and came round to the front again.

'I've bought petrol here before.'

The words tripped easily from Diana's lips, but seeing the expression on Adam's face she wished she had laughed the whole thing off and not lied. Yet though annoyed with herself, she was more annoyed with Adam for allowing her to believe... But what had he allowed her to believe? Nothing, if she was honest about it. He had said he was studying electronics—as he probably was—and she had assumed he was a full-time student. Could this be his father's garage, and he was helping him in his spare time? She longed to ask him, but aware of Jane beside her, remained silent. What rotten luck she hadn't come here alone.

She was debating whether to tell Jane the truth when Adam spoke.

'Credit card or cash, miss?' He was standing by the window, stony-faced, but the flare of his nostrils showed her the 'miss' was barbed.

'Cash,' she said quickly, anxious to leave.

Pressing twenty pounds into his hand, and not waiting for the change, she drove off. Only as she reached the end of the forecourt did she silently admit she could not leave without apologising, and abruptly drew to a stop.

'I want to get some mints,' she excused herself, and jumped out.

Adam was filling a Volvo as she reached his side, and though he glanced at her, he did not speak.

'I'm sorry I didn't introduce you to my friend,' she said breathlessly. 'But I——'

'Forget it. *I* have.'

He turned away and Diana watched him uncertainly.

'Come on, Diana,' Jane called. 'The man behind us can't get past.'

Pink-cheeked, Diana touched Adam's arm. 'About Thursday. Can you make it seven, not seven-fifteen?'

'Come on!' Jane called again.

Giving him a brief smile, Diana dashed to her car.

For the rest of that day and the next she rehearsed what to say to Adam when they met, aware that the apology she had proffered at the garage was inadequate. Yet though she thought of several pretty speeches, none explained away her appalling behaviour. The only solution was to admit it and ask him to forgive her.

Having reached her decision, she felt easier in her mind, though she was still nervous as she stood in the foyer of the Festival Hall waiting for him to arrive. She had dressed carefully, discarding designer labels for a comparatively inexpensive white and navy silk shirt, matching cardigan and navy culottes, purchased while on holiday in Spain.

If only he'd get here, she thought, her nervousness growing as seven o'clock came and went, and seven-fifteen gave way to the half-hour. At eight o'clock, with the concert well under way and the foyer deserted, she knew she had been stood up.

Anger swamped her. Clearly he had meant to humiliate her as she had humiliated him. It was a pettiness she had not expected from him, and flinging the tickets to the floor she headed home.

Her night was restless as she tossed and turned, discarding various ways of getting her own back. No one had ever stood her up before, and she was damned if she'd let him get away with it.

Next morning she was ready to go out by nine-thirty, much to her mother's surprise.

'It isn't your morning for being at the florist, is it, darling?'

'No. But Jane wants me to help her look for a new dress,' she lied, and gulping down her coffee, rushed out. She was in a foul mood and would continue to be until she had seen Adam Brooke and told him exactly what she thought of him.

Her ill-humour increased as she reached the garage and saw the line of cars ahead of her. Parking by the kerb, she went into the shop, deciding it was easier to speak to Adam there than outside, where he was surrounded by customers.

Through the window she watched him. She was positive he had seen her come in, though he had given no sign of it, and her impatience grew as the two cars he filled were paid off with the exact amount of money, which he stuffed into the pocket of his overalls.

'If you don't soon come in,' she muttered, 'I'll come out and throttle you!'

Almost as if the next customer had heard her, she saw him produce a credit card, and hand it to Adam.

'About time too,' she said clearly as he came in and walked over to the counter. 'Aren't you going to say anything?'

'Good morning,' he said calmly.

'Don't "good morning" me as if nothing's wrong! How dare you stand me up?'

He looked at the card in his hand, picked up a pen and began writing the receipt.

'Didn't you hear me?' she insisted.

Only then did he look at her again. 'You got what you deserved.'

'I said I was sorry. What else do you want?'

'Nothing—from you. You're a spoiled little rich girl who doesn't know how to behave. Stick to your own

kind, then you won't have anything to be ashamed of.'
Credit card and receipt in hand, he went to the door.

'I'm not ashamed of you,' she said, barring his way.

'You could have fooled me.'

'I was surprised to see you working here and I——'

'Decided you didn't know me.' He moved around her.
'I'm not angry with you, and I appreciate you coming
back to apologise. Now be a good girl and go home.'

'Don't talk to me as if I were a child,' she snapped.

'But you are.'

'Then treat me like one and forgive me,' she said instantly, her large sapphire eyes imploring him.

He shook his head and went out, leaving her close to
tears. In spite of his lack of temper, she knew she had
hurt him deeply, and her anger towards him dissolved,
leaving her angry only with herself.

'Still here?' he questioned as he returned with another
credit card.

'I'm staying until you promise to meet me for lunch
and let me explain.'

'There's nothing for you to explain.'

'Meet me anyway.'

'I don't have a lunch break.'

'Then I'll collect you when you finish work. *Please.*'

She moved a step closer, breathing in the warmth
emanating from him, and aware of herself in a way she
had never before experienced. She didn't know why he
had this effect on her; all she knew was that she didn't
want him to think badly of her.

'You can be as rude to me as you like,' she added
humbly. 'I deserve it.'

For several seconds he stared at her, then he sighed.
'I go to evening school every night, but I can meet you
at nine-thirty at Camden Town station.'

'It's the other side of London!'

'Not for me.' His tone was dry. 'If you want to forget it...'

'No, I'll be there.' She walked with him across the forecourt. 'You won't stand me up again, will you?'

'Enjoy yourself guessing,' he replied, and walked towards his waiting customer.

CHAPTER THREE

DIANA spent the rest of the day regretting the arrangement she had made with Adam. She must need her head examined to traipse halfway across London to see a man who made it clear he couldn't care less if he never saw her again.

Yet nine o'clock found her doing exactly that, and scared she'd be late as well, for she had put on and taken off two different outfits before finally deciding on a third. The last thing she wanted was to look the spoilt little rich girl he had accused her of being. She had gone easy on her make-up too, wearing only a lip gloss and a touch of mascara to darken her long, thick lashes, and pulling her hair into a pony-tail: a deliberate ploy to look younger than she was in the hope of disarming him.

Despite driving fast, she was ten minutes late before she had parked her car in a side turning and reached the station entrance. There was no sign of Adam and she stopped dead. He had stood her up again! The pang of hurt that stabbed her surprised her by its intensity, making her realise she desperately wanted to go on seeing him.

A throng of people emerged from the station, and as it thinned she saw Adam walking along the pavement. Joy filled her and she moved towards him, slowing her step as she noticed he hadn't quickened his. Wasn't he even a little pleased to see her?

'I thought you'd given me a taste of my own medicine,' he said as he reached her side.

'Medicine?'

'That you'd stood me up.'

'But you've only just got here,' she said indignantly.

His face lit with a smile that softened the stern set of his features and made him look younger than the mid-twenties she guessed him to be.

'Where do we go from here?' she asked happily, and seeing his startled expression knew he had read more into her question than she had meant. It startled her too, making her ponder on where their relationship could lead. But she pushed it aside. Why think of the future when the present was so exciting?

'My car's parked round the corner,' she went on. 'Shall we drive to the West End or find a place for coffee round here?'

'I thought we'd go on a boat,' he answered.

'A boat?' She glanced round the dingy streets, thinking he was joking.

'We're not far from Camden Lock,' he explained, 'and we can go from there to Regent's Park and back in under an hour.'

'Sounds great,' she said, not having a clue what he was talking about.

He made no conversation as they walked, and after several minutes she felt it was up to her to start the ball rolling. Unfortunately, short of apologising once more for her behaviour at the garage, she could not find anything to say. It was strange for her to be lost for words, when she was known for her quick tongue and sharp wit. Yet she knew instinctively that what her friends might consider funny, Adam wouldn't, and the knowledge made her self-conscious.

'Have we much further to go?' she questioned.

'We're nearly there.' He nodded towards the next turning, and as they rounded it she saw it was a narrow street leading to a jetty. Because of the lateness of the hour it was not surprising to find only a few people waiting to buy tickets for the white-painted boat. Wryly wondering if he expected her to pay for herself, she slowed her step, pleased as he walked past her and bought two tickets.

'It's usually very crowded,' he said, putting a hand under her elbow to help her aboard.

'The forecast was rain,' Diana replied.

'Maybe that's why.'

She nodded. What a pain if they could talk only of the weather. He doesn't want to be with me, she thought, and though dismayed by the knowledge, determined not to let him know she was aware of it. He led her to the stern of the boat, which was empty, and they sat down as it began to chug slowly along the canal.

'I take it you haven't done this before,' Adam said.

'I've only been on the Thames.'

'This is a first for me too.'

'Really?'

'Why the surprise?'

She shrugged. 'I imagined you often brought your dates here.'

'I rarely date.'

'By inclination or design?'

'A bit of both. I'm too busy for one thing, and for another I prefer to save my money.'

'I bet plenty of girls would go Dutch with you.'

He laughed, a deep sound that brought her eyes instantly to his chest and the muscles rippling beneath his open-necked shirt. His sleeves were rolled back and she saw how strong his arms were, with fine dark hairs lightly covering them. It was his hands that held her gaze longest: they were powerful, with square-tipped fingers, the nails cut short. Hard to believe he worked in a garage and had them dirty most of the day.

'What are you thinking?' he demanded.

'How clean your hands are,' she blurted out.

'Detergent and a tough nail-brush.'

There was amusement in his voice, and a softness that had not been there before, which made her feel happy again.

'About the other day...' Hesitantly she raised the subject, knowing she had to clear the air. 'You were right. I was too ashamed to introduce you to Jane.'

'Thanks for being honest. Now let's forget it.'

Silence fell between them, but this time she didn't find it an uncomfortable one.

'Why do you work at the garage?' she asked finally.

'Art lovers have to earn a living too! Or are the men you know as idle as the girls?'

'None of my friends is idle.'

'I bet none of them has to work to eat.'

'Are you always so defensive?'

He regarded her in surprise, then frowned as he considered her question. 'Not usually. It's just that I haven't gone out with anyone like you before.'

'By that, I assume you mean rich?'

'Yes.'

'Then we're both in the same boat—metaphorically and physically! I've never been out with anyone like *you*.'

He grinned, and seemed so relaxed that she decided to ask him the question that had been bothering her from the beginning.

'Why didn't you study electronics when you left school, instead of waiting until now? Or hadn't you made up your mind what you wanted to do?'

'All I ever wanted was to earn money. I was brought up in a children's home and used to count the days till I was free to leave.'

'How awful for you. Were you terribly unhappy there?'

'No,' he said abruptly. 'But I counted the days till I could leave and be independent. Once I was in the real world I realised that if I wanted to better myself, I had to have a profession or a trade.'

'Why did you choose electronics?'

'Because it's a growing industry.'

'I see.' She hesitated. 'Do you remember your parents?'

'My mother dumped me when I was a baby and disappeared. As for Father...' Adam shrugged. 'I doubt if my mother knew who he was.'

'It must be awful not having any family,' Diana sympathised.

'You get used to it,' he said dismissively. 'The home I was in was fine, and I don't think I missed out on much.'

You missed out on love, Diana thought, her heart going out to him. How very different his life had been from hers.

Unexpectedly he reached for her hand, running calloused fingers over the soft skin and long, polished nails. 'Tell me about *you*, and how you keep the wolf from the door—or should I say mink?'

'You're always on the defensive,' she accused. 'Even when you make a joke you have to be rude.'

'You're right,' he admitted instantly. 'I'll rephrase the question. What do you do with yourself each day when you're not making some young man happy batting those lovely long eyelashes at him?'

'I'm at a local florist part-time.'

'How appropriate. A perfect English rose selling flowers!'

'Roses can have sharp thorns.'

'Is that a warning?'

'Maybe.'

'I've a tough skin,' he replied. 'A few thorns won't worry me.' He let her fingers slide through his, then placed her hand back in her lap.

He fell silent, and she looked out over the water. It was dark, shadowed by the trees and bushes that bordered the canal walk, and lit only by the reflection of street lamps.

'We've passed the zoo,' Adam commented. 'I bet you haven't been there either.'

'Yes, I have. My nanny often took me.'

'That figures,' he grunted, and seeing her mouth tighten, added, 'Sorry—I was getting at you, wasn't I?'

'You do it on purpose. But I'll forgive you if you answer a few more questions.'

'Fire away.'

'How old are you?'

'Twenty-six.'

'How much longer before you qualify?'

'A few more months. I've been offered an excellent job—providing my results are good.'

'I'm sure they will be.'

'I hope so. I'm studying damned hard.' His jaw clenched. 'I've so much to do and very little time.'

'What's the rush?'

'I want to have money while I'm young enough to enjoy it.'

'I see,' Diana said uncomfortably. She had never bothered about money, and found it hard to imagine not having enough to do what one wanted.

'Do you?' he asked sharply.

'Of course. It's great to be ambitious.'

'I'm glad you approve. If you hadn't, I'd have gone back to digging ditches.'

Diana went scarlet, aware she had sounded condescending. 'Did you really dig ditches?'

'My sweet little innocent.' His anger left him as quickly as it had risen. 'You have no idea what life is all about, have you?' With rough tenderness he caught her by the shoulders and pulled her towards him, his eyes ranging over her face as if itemising every feature. 'I've dug ditches and mended roads, hauled garbage and cleaned sewers. In fact, anything that kept me from the dole queue. Being in the garage is coming up in the world, I can tell you!'

'I'm sorry. I didn't mean to——'

'Don't keep apologising,' he rebuked gently. 'I don't expect you to understand my world, any more than I understand yours. That's why I figured it was best if I didn't see you.'

'But you did,' she whispered, and put her arms around his neck with a boldness that astonished her, for normally she expected a man to do all the running. But with Adam it was different. With him she had no inhibitions. 'Kiss me,' she pleaded. 'Please kiss me.'

She pulled his head down, and though he resisted as she touched her lips to his, he muttered deep in his throat and lowered his mouth to hers. At the feel of his mouth she shivered with desire and knew a violent longing to hold him close for ever. How vulnerable he was despite his self-assured manner; so vulnerable that she ached to protect him. Eagerly she pressed closer to him, but as he felt the softness of her body he thrust her so sharply away that she almost fell off the seat.

'Sorry,' he said thickly, his arm coming out to steady her, 'but it isn't my night to be seduced.'

'You should be so lucky!' she snapped, and saw his eyes narrow with surprise before he pulled her close again.

This time he was the one to take command, his kisses hard and demanding, his lips forcing hers apart to give his tongue entry. It was an intimacy she rarely allowed, and certainly not on a first date. Yet she found herself willingly responding to him, her tongue entwining with his, their movements simulating the movements of a greater intimacy. His hands caressed her shoulders and her back, grasping her small waist and bringing her body hard against his, so that she felt the pounding of his heart. Or was it hers? What matter? She felt as if they were one.

'No,' he gasped, and for the second time pushed her away. 'It won't work, Diana. It's no good kidding ourselves. We've nothing in common.'

'If that were true, we wouldn't be here.'

'Put it down to sexual attraction.'

Diana knew there was more to it than that. She stared into his face and saw the features illumined by a passing street lamp. It picked out the strong nose and beautifully chiselled mouth; made dark sockets of his eyes and silvered the edges of his thick, unruly hair.

Was she falling in love with him? He was certainly the most interesting man she had met. More exciting too; and there was no way she was going to let him walk out of her life without putting up a fight.

Her emotion must have communicated itself to him, for he drew one finger along the curve of her cheek. She caught hold of his hand and put it to her lips, then slid across the seat and rested her head upon his chest. His heart was beating fast, and she delighted in the knowledge that she could arouse him so easily.

'We're back where we started,' Adam said, pulling her to her feet, and she was startled to see that the boat had returned to Camden Lock. 'I don't know about you, blondie, but I'm starving.'

'Me too,' she murmured, realising she was. 'But it's my turn to pay.'

'Not with me, you don't.'

'That's stupid. These days, girls often——'

'When we see each other, *I* pay. Take it or leave it.'

'I'll take it,' she said quickly as they walked on to the jetty. Expecting him to make a joking reply, she was taken aback when he stopped walking and faced her.

'You've definitely addled my brain. A moment ago I said I wasn't going to see you again.'

'It's not solely a woman's prerogative to change her mind,' she teased.

'This is the first time *I've* ever done so.' He shook his head. 'I wish I understood why.'

'Because I'm brilliant, blonde and beautiful!'

'I've met other beautiful women,' he muttered. 'But there's something about you that... I must be out of my mind.'

With a sudden laugh she stood on tiptoe and pressed her lips to his. 'We're both out of our minds, Adam, but isn't it a wonderful place to be?'

CHAPTER FOUR

'REALLY, Diana,' Mrs Farrow exclaimed. 'Why on earth do you want us to have dinner in the breakfast-room?'

'Because only Adam is coming, and the dining-room is too big and formal.'

'I've invited Angela and Mark as well.'

'Oh, Mother, you haven't! They're such prigs. If I'd known, I'd have asked Adam another night.' Diana tried to imagine him with her two cousins, and groaned. 'All they talk about are horses.'

'What's wrong with that? I'm sure your friend rides.'

Diana hid a smile, imagining her mother's reaction if she learned that the only thing he rode was a second-hand motorbike.

'What does he actually do?' her mother went on. 'The only Brookes I know are a charming couple your father and I met on the cruise last year. They have a place near Glastonbury.'

'I doubt if they're related,' Diana replied, and hurriedly changed the subject.

She had been wary of asking Adam home, as much concerned with his response to her parents as theirs to him. But because of her behaviour at the garage she was anxious to show him she wasn't the snob he believed her to be. And what better way than by introducing him to her parents?

Although her mother came from a titled family, her father's background was middle-class, and he had become wealthy through ability and hard work. Indeed, whenever his wife pretended he had inherited his money, he would favour his daughter with a wink.

'Don't be tough on your mother because she's a bit of a snob,' he had once reprimanded her. 'She came from the top drawer but it was a pretty empty one—that's why she sets such store by position and money.'

'Is that why she married you?' Diana had asked with the brutal frankness of a fifteen-year-old.

'No, my nosy one! When we met, I was just setting up in business and didn't even have a car. We married for love, and I hope you will do the same.'

'Does she get depressions because she was poor as a child?'

'No. It has more to do with her mother dying when she was born and her father packing her off to boarding-school when she was six. That's why she's so loving with *you*. She wants you to have the affection *she* never had.'

It was an affection Diana had frequently found smothering, though her father's explanation had given her a greater understanding of it, as it had also done of the black moods that sometimes lasted a few days, and sometimes necessitated her mother's stay in a nursing home.

'Diana, do stop dreaming!' Mrs Farrow brought her swiftly back to the present. 'I asked if you'd like Cook to prepare anything special for dinner?'

'Whatever Carmen makes will be delicious.'

In no mood for further talk about the dinner party, Diana pretended she had a telephone call to make, and went out. She was very much on edge, uncertain how Adam would react to her parents and her home. Though not ostentatious it had all the trappings of wealth, and emphasised the difference between them; a difference that worried him however much she tried to reassure him it didn't worry *her*.

'I bet you'd like me to put on a dinner-jacket?' he had teased.

'My father often does,' she had answered laconically. 'But only if it's a special affair.'

'And your mother sports a tiara, I suppose!'

'Only when she does the washing-up!'

'I bet she's never been near a sink,' he had grunted, and knowing this to be true, Diana had not answered.

She recollected this as she hovered in the hall that evening, waiting for him to arrive. As she saw his silhouette through the side window, she shushed away Mario, the butler-handyman who was Carmen's husband, and opened the door herself.

Never had she seen him so handsome or so formally attired. Brown wool trousers and a linen jacket of the same colour matched his chestnut-brown eyes and thick glossy hair. He had taken a firm brush to it, she noticed with amazement, for the errant waves were flat, though there was still a suggestion of curl at the side of his neck. He wore a tie too—wonders would never cease!—and it dawned on her that despite his casual acceptance of her invitation, he had gone to considerable trouble to dress up for it. She hoped he hadn't bought the clothes especially, but knew that even if he had he wouldn't allow her to reimburse him.

Lightly touching his arm, she led him into the drawing-room, and watching the polite yet friendly way he greeted her parents, she was filled with pride. He cut a far better figure than her cousin Mark, who he topped by a head, a fact that her cousin Angela was quick to notice, for she joined Adam on the settee, preventing Diana from doing so.

Standing slightly apart from everyone, she saw the scene as a set piece that might have graced a Noel Coward play. Not that there was anything Noel Cowardish in the way her father steered the conversation to the current

Test match, a subject dear to Adam's heart, and within moments the three men were absorbed.

'I like your new boyfriend,' Angela murmured, coming to stand beside her. 'Where did you meet him?'

'At the Tate.'

Angela's reply was drowned by Mario informing them that dinner was served, and as they went into the dining-room, Diana saw it through Adam's eyes: the long rosewood table that comfortably seated thirty, the silver place settings, and the three silver and gold bowls filled with flowers that ranged along its dark surface.

He gave no sign of being overawed by his sur-roundings, though as their glances met across the table she saw amusement in the quirk of his mouth, and had the impression he knew exactly what was going through her mind.

Angela, seated on his left, started to question him. 'Diana said you met at the Tate. Does that mean you're an artist?'

'One doesn't have to be an artist to go to the Tate,' he countered, his serious expression belying the glint in his eyes.

'Well, no, but—er—is painting your hobby then?'

'I haven't time for hobbies, but I'm interested in art.'

'Adam's studying electronic engineering,' Diana intervened.

'I'm hopeless at anything mechanical,' Angela exclaimed.

'I'm sure you can do many other things,' Adam said.

'Riding, mostly. And I adore skiing. Do you?'

'I've never tried it.'

'Where do you holiday in the winter?'

Diana held her breath, expelling it with relief as Adam said, 'I don't take holidays. I'm working too hard.'

'You ride though?' This from Mark, whose tone in-dicated that no one could live without a horse.

'Riding isn't everyone's idea of fun,' Diana interjected.

'I suppose it depends on one's school,' Angela added. 'Mine favoured tennis and swimming. What about yours, Di?'

'The same,' she answered, thinking this was a tricky subject too, and her heart jolted as Mark posed the question to Adam.

'The local comprehensive,' he replied.

'How terribly progressive,' Angela gushed. 'I do admire people who go to government schools.'

'I don't,' her brother commented. 'A boarding-school teaches one reliance.'

'I wouldn't want strangers bringing up *my* children,' Adam stated. 'I think it's a lazy way of having a family.'

'More wine?' Diana cut in, and as Mario obliged, deliberately changed the conversation.

The evening proceeded normally, though there was a distinct cooling off in Angela's attitude to Adam. It seemed that not even his good looks were sufficient compensation for his blunt comments!

Coffee was served in the drawing-room, and Adam declined a brandy or liqueur, saying hard spirits made him tired and he had to be up early in the morning.

'Does it matter if you miss a lecture?' Mark queried.

'It's not a lecture I'd miss, it's my job. I start at seven.'

'But aren't you at university?' Mrs Farrow asked, puzzled.

'I'm studying at night school,' Adam explained, 'and during the day I work in a garage.'

'Family-owned?'

'Adam doesn't believe in nepotism,' Diana put in hastily.

'Very commendable,' her father agreed. 'It's good for your character to make your own way in the world.'

'I had no choice,' Adam said. 'I——'

'Another coffee, anyone?' Diana interposed.

'Not for me,' Mark said. 'Angela and I must be going. We're driving down to Wiltshire tonight.'

Hiding her delight at their early departure, she almost pushed them to the door. With her cousins gone, the risk of Adam putting his foot in it was considerably lessened. Of course there would come a time when she wouldn't be able to stop him, but by then she hoped her parents would have come to appreciate what a wonderful person he was, and how much he meant to her.

'I've an early call too,' her father announced as she sat down on the sofa. 'So if you two youngsters will excuse me...'

Her mother followed him, flashing her a meaningful warning as she did.

'Does that glare your mother gave you mean it's time I left?' Adam questioned, running his hands through his hair and ruffling the flat waves into its usual attractive unruliness.

'Not this instant.' Diana kicked off her shoes and lolled back on the sofa. 'You're allowed half an hour's grace.'

He said nothing, nor did he take the hint to leave his chair and sit next to her. She waited for him to speak but he appeared content to remain silent, and she swallowed her irritation.

'I hope my cousins didn't bore you?' she murmured.

'They were OK. How come you're so different from them when you have similar backgrounds?'

'I'm an individual, not a clone. And from your comment, I take it you didn't like them.'

'You're right,' he said bluntly, and loosened his tie as though unaccustomed to its constriction. 'If you're spoiling for a fight, I'll go.'

'That's right. Use any excuse to leave,' she stormed, her anxiety of the past few hours exploding into temper. 'I'm amazed you agreed to come here at all. We're so obviously beneath you in brains and intelligence!'

'You said it, not me.'

Infuriated by his conceit, she glared at him, and unexpectedly he chuckled.

'Don't you know when you're being teased?'

'Not when I'm with *you*.' Her temper dissolved, swamped by sadness. 'I never know where I am with you.'

'I'm sorry, Di. But I learned the hard way that it's better to hide your feelings.'

'Even from a person you care about?' She waited for his answer, but he leaned back in his chair and stared into space. If he had behaved like this when they had first met she would have been resentful, but the little she had learned of him enabled her to see below the surface to the emotionally complex man he was. Being silent was his reaction when he didn't know what to do or was uncertain of himself.

Rising, she moved over to his chair and perched on the arm, swinging one shapely leg provocatively. 'I think Angela fancied you.'

'You mean she fancied the common touch!'

Diana changed the subject. 'My father liked you.'

'Don't give me that! Tonight wasn't a disaster but it was a near miss. Every time I opened my mouth you looked terrified in case I put my foot in it.'

'That isn't true,' she lied. 'I didn't want anyone upsetting you.'

'People who don't matter to me can't upset me,' he said bluntly.

'What an arrogant thing to say! I'm glad you aren't rich or you'd be insufferable.'

For a startled instant he stared at her. Then he flung back his head and laughed, at the same time pulling her down on to his lap.

'What a kid you are,' he muttered, and drawing her face close, covered her mouth with his.

It was a fierce kiss, forcing her lips brutally apart and invading the soft interior. Momentarily she resisted, but as always, desire swamped her, a hot curling flame that trembled from her stomach to her thighs and along every limb. Desperately she pressed herself against him, as if by so doing she could become part of him.

With a hoarse cry he tore his mouth from hers and stood up, setting her on her feet before he strode over to the window and pulled the curtain aside to stare out into the night.

Blankly she stared at his back, her desire slowly ebbing, leaving her feeling strangely desolate.

'What is it?' she whispered. 'Have I done something wrong?'

'It isn't you, it's me.' He swung round on her. 'I shouldn't be here, Di, and you know it. We've no future together.'

'How can you say that? Don't I mean anything to you?'

'Too much. That's why I can't let you go on living in a fool's paradise. The timing is wrong for us, Di. Maybe if we meet ten years on—but not now, when I've nothing to offer you. Can't you see that?'

Angrily she turned away from him. Of course she saw it. She wasn't stupid! She also saw that it didn't matter; her father was rich enough to give him all the help he needed. But she knew better than to say it. She had to lead up to it carefully, for he was proud and wouldn't readily accept help.

The thought of this angered her. If he truly loved her he would be willing to do anything to keep her in his life. Her anger increased. Adam was no weakling who gave up at the first obstacle, but a strong man determined to get what he wanted. And apparently, he didn't want her. At least not enough to fight for her. Well, to hell with him! Who was *he* to turn her down?

'I'm sorry,' he muttered. 'The last thing I want is to hurt you.'

'You haven't. I think you're right—we shouldn't meet again. You're so weighed down by that chip on your shoulder, you can't afford to be burdened with other worries. I'm sorry I wasted so much of your valuable time.'

A flush marked his cheekbones and his mouth narrowed, drawing attention to the lines either side of it, which spoke of long hours of hard work. Seeing them, she nearly flung herself into his arms and told him how much she loved him. Nearly, but didn't.

'Knowing you wasn't a waste,' he said quietly. 'Parting from you is the waste.' His hand came out as if to touch her, then dropped to his side. 'Goodbye, blondie.'

Afraid of giving herself away, she turned her back on him, and didn't move until the click of the front door announced his departure. Only then did she come to life, storming up to her room and showering in water so hot that it burned her skin. Yet it didn't burn away the pain of rejection; any more than the strong mint taste of her toothpaste could eradicate the sweetness of his mouth.

With a cry she flung herself on the bed and burst into tears. She couldn't bear life without him, and was bitterly hurt that he had been able to walk away from *her*.

'But I can be as determined as you, Adam Brooke,' she said aloud, and hearing the resolution in her voice, gained strength from it. 'You may be cleverer than I am, but I'll find a way of getting round you.'

Recalling how his body had trembled at her touch, she realised where her power lay. Yet she had to use it with subtlety, and that would take careful planning.

CHAPTER FIVE

'DIANA, wake up!'

A sharp, insistent voice aroused a reluctant Diana from a deep sleep, and she opened her eyes to find her mother standing at the foot of her bed. 'What's wrong?'

'I want to talk to you.'

'Can't it wait till later?' she muttered, slowly un-curling her body and stretching soft slim arms above her head.

'No, it can't. It's about that young man you invited here last night. Your father and I don't want you to see him again.'

Diana was instantly wide awake. 'Why not?'

'Is it necessary for me to tell you?'

'Yes, it is. He's educated, intelligent and hard-working. What else do you want?'

'I'm sure he's a very nice young man, dear, but he isn't right for you. And don't give me that innocent look. You know exactly what I mean. If——' Her mother broke off as the door opened and her husband entered, dapper in grey pin-stripes.

'My two girls arguing?' he asked jovially.

'I've been telling Diana we don't want her to continue seeing this—whatever his name is.'

'Adam Brooke,' Diana put in sharply, 'and stop pretending you don't remember it.'

'No need to lose your temper, poppet,' her father reproved, joining his wife at the foot of the bed. 'Your mother's right. Adam is a fine young man but he's in no position to settle down.'

'You're nineteen, and this is the best time of your life,' Mrs Farrow added. 'You should be out enjoying yourself, not wasting time on a nobody.'

'What a rotten thing to say!' Diana cried. 'Being poor doesn't make you a nobody.'

'Your mother didn't mean it the way it sounded,' her father placated, placing a cautionary hand on his wife's arm. 'These days, people are judged on what they are, not who their parents were. And quite right too. But that still doesn't make Adam right for you. You come from different worlds, and he's intelligent enough to realise it.'

'If he did, he wouldn't have come here last night,' Mrs Farrow sniffed.

'Perhaps he enjoys slumming!' Diana retorted sarcastically.

'That's enough!' her father said, and recognising the authority in his voice, she held her tongue. 'We'll wait breakfast for you,' he went on. 'Don't be long.'

Diana was in control of herself when she joined her parents in the sunny breakfast-room off the conservatory. It was fragrant with the aroma of freshly ground Blue Mountain and freshly made toast, but the thought of food nauseated her and she filled her cup and perched on a chair.

'Well,' she said, 'what else do you have to say?'

'Only things that are for your own good,' her father said quietly. 'As I said before, Adam seems a decent young man, but he has a long way to go before he has made something of his life, and if you continue going out with him it will give him ideas.'

'Above his station, you mean?'

'That isn't what I meant, my dear, and you know it. In a few years, when he has established himself, I wouldn't have any objection to you seeing him, but——'

'But now you must stop!' Mrs Farrow cut in exasperatedly. 'Otherwise you'll fall in love with him and make a fool of yourself...'

I'm already in love with him, Diana wanted to say defiantly, and as the words came into her mind, she knew with startling clarity that they were true. It had nothing to do with proving her power over him. She loved him and wanted to marry him.

'...so it's for the best,' her mother finished.

'The best?' Diana echoed, not having heard a word that had been said.

'That you go and stay with Aunt Leona. You've never been to the States and she's always inviting you. Three months in Virginia will be fun, and your father and I will come over for Christmas and take you skiing in Aspen.'

'And buy me a teddy bear too?' Diana asked sharply.

'We're not your enemies, Didi,' her father cut in, using his pet name for her, which she thought was hitting below the belt. 'We want your happiness and we think it best if you distance yourself from Adam.'

'And if I refuse?'

'We hope you won't.'

Pushing back her chair, Diana stalked out. She had been given an ultimatum and had to think it over.

Although Adam himself had said they should stop seeing each other, she was positive she could persuade him to change his mind. But if she went to America for three months their relationship was too fragile to withstand such a lengthy separation.

The urge to see him was so strong that within the hour she was in her car heading for the garage. Only as the petrol pumps came into view did her confidence ebb. What if he insisted he meant what he had said last night? She turned into the forecourt and drew up. An attendant approached and she said she wanted to speak to Adam.

Grinning appreciatively, he took in Diana's shining corn-gold hair and sun-kissed skin. 'He's in the office. I'll go tell him.'

He ambled into the small stucco building at the back of the forecourt, and a moment later came out again, waved at her, then disappeared into the bowels of a Ford. Of Adam there was no sign.

Ten minutes passed and she stirred restlessly. Her inclination was to go in search of him but she restrained herself, certain he was deliberately keeping her waiting. But when a quarter of an hour had passed she wondered if there was a back entrance to the office through which he might have escaped. Yet from her reading of his character it was hard to envisage him skulking off to avoid her. He was more the type to face her. Yet if so, where on earth was he?

She had half opened the car door when he emerged from the office. As always at sight of him, any annoyance or anger she was experiencing was superseded by joy. And today it was stronger than ever, heightened by the fear of being parted from him. I can't give him up, she thought. No matter what my parents say, I'm going to fight for him.

As Adam drew nearer she noticed the tight set of his jaw. 'Don't you ever give up?' he asked as he reached her window.

'Not as easily as you. I fight for what I want.'

He reddened, and the hardness that filled his face gave her an inkling of how he might look after a few years of fighting for the success he was determined to have. Even now the gentle facets of his character were being swamped by his driving ambition, and if there was no love in his life while he was striving to get to the top, then ten years from now—that was the time he had given himself to succeed—he would be too shrivelled emotionally to respond to love when it came his way.

'Do you want petrol?' he said. 'If not, you're blocking the forecourt for nothing.'

'Don't be rude.'

'Then quit wasting my time. I'm working here, Diana, not hosting a lunch party.'

'Can't you take an hour off? I want to talk to you.'

'We said it all last night.'

'You said it—I didn't get a chance.'

'Whatever you say won't change my mind. Now do you mind going? I've a lot on my plate today.'

Whatever he had on his plate didn't compare with what her parents had dished out to *her* this morning, though she knew better than to say so.

'How about later this afternoon?' she asked quietly. 'What time do you finish today?'

'Four.'

'Then perhaps we can go somewhere quiet and talk. Your place?'

He eyed her lemon silk suit, casual in cut but clearly expensive. 'I don't think my beat-up leather armchair will make a fitting background for you.'

'That's your hang-up, Adam—not mine.'

'Maybe, but it's how I feel.' He ran his hand down the side of his cheek, leaving a grease mark along it, and she was convinced he had done it deliberately to show her how far apart their worlds were.

'You can always ask me back to your place,' he went on.

She hated the sarcasm in his voice but this was no time to tell him. Other things took precedence.

'My parents are giving a party,' she lied, 'and the house is teeming with caterers and florists.'

'How come you aren't doing the flowers?'

She was at a loss what to say, and stared at him helplessly.

Adam sighed. 'If you're so desperate to talk, we can go to a café round the corner.'

A tête-à-tête in a noisy café wasn't what she had planned. She wanted to be alone with him; to use her charms to disarm him—and anything else it might take to persuade him to continue their relationship. Suddenly she thought of Hugo Hemming, Jane's brother, who had a luxurious bachelor pad by the river in Chelsea Wharf.

'He's gone to the States for a month,' Jane had confided last week, 'and he deputed me to water his precious plants. You can't imagine how the place is decorated. It's absolutely decadent! Mirrored ceilings, leather everywhere, and one of those fabulous round beds. If you fancy taking a peep...'

Well, now was as good a time as any, Diana decided, though without Jane in tow.

'I know a place where we can talk alone,' she said to Adam. 'Is it OK if I call to give you the address?'

He nodded, looking less than thrilled, and without so much as a goodbye walked off. She glared at his back, wondering why she was bothering to run after a man who didn't give a damn whether he saw her or not. Yet it was this *laissez-faire* attitude that impelled her to do so; a determination to make him admit she had got beneath his skin and that he wanted her.

And when she had, what then? Would she still want *him*? Since leaving finishing school she had had innumerable crushes on men in her circle, but Adam was the first man she had ever fancied who had played hard to get.

Swinging her car back on to the road, she made for the estate office in Knightsbridge where Jane worked, though since it was her brother's firm, her hours were elastic.

At first her friend was reluctant to give her the key of her brother's apartment, particularly when she discovered who Diana was taking there, but eventually she agreed, though not before adding a salutary warning for her to be careful.

At the first phone-box she came to, Diana called Adam and gave him the Chelsea address.

'Whose place is it?' he asked.

'It belongs to my girlfriend's brother—and we can be alone there and talk.'

'I don't think it's a good idea.'

'Please,' she begged. 'If you don't want to see me after today I swear I won't bother you again.'

'Very well. I'll be there about four.'

Pleased that things were going her way, Diana went home to fetch her tennis gear, then set off for the Queens Club, where one of London's top coaches was waiting to put her through her paces.

It was lunchtime before she was home again. Her father had long since left for his office and her mother was at one of her inevitable bridge lunches. Relieved not to be pestered about Adam, Diana munched an apple, then rummaged through her wardrobe, considering what to wear. Adam would have a fit if he saw her wall-length cupboards full of designer clothes, nearly every outfit costing more than he earned in a month!

Moving to a rack of cotton dresses, she chose a simple blue one—didn't they say men were suckers for blue? She barely used any make-up either, and her hair, still damp from her shower, swung softly around her ears, giving her the air of a medieval pageboy. But not too much of the boy, she admitted, eyeing the firm tilt of her breasts as she turned to pick up her purse before going downstairs.

It was three o'clock when she entered Hugo's apartment, heart pounding as though she was a thief. As indeed she was, though the object she was intent on stealing was a man; a proud, wary man who was fighting to resist her.

To calm her nerves she wandered through the rooms, amused by the vast sunken tub in the bathroom, with its gilded taps in the shape of a naked woman. The bedroom was also clearly that of a bachelor, with everything electronically operated from a panel by the king-sized bed, draped in simulated leopardskin.

If Adam had the money would he indulge himself in a similar fashion? She doubted it, for his down-to-earth attitude precluded such fantasies, in spite of his strong sexuality. Impatiently she glanced at her watch. Not quite four. He should be here soon unless he had changed his mind. The notion was enough to knot her stomach, and she winced with the pain.

'Please God, make him come,' she said aloud. 'I love him so much, and I need this chance to show him.'

CHAPTER SIX

When the front doorbell finally chimed, Diana walked slowly across to answer it, showing no sign of her inner turmoil as she greeted Adam.

'Your friend's brother must enjoy looking at himself,' he commented from the threshold, taking in the mirrored hall and the living-room beyond it.

'I don't think it's just himself he likes to look at!' she giggled. 'Wait till you see the bedroom.' She ran across and flung open the door.

Adam strolled after her and peered inside. 'It's like a set in a pornographic movie!'

'I wouldn't know about that.'

'Keep it that way. You haven't missed a thing.'

'Have you seen many?'

'A couple. But I wouldn't want to see any more.'

She swallowed her curiosity. 'Care for a coffee?'

He nodded and followed her to the kitchen, leaning against the lintel and folding his arms across his chest. He dwarfed the small area and looked very masculine among the blue and white cabinets. Knowing he was watching her, Diana was all fingers and thumbs.

'Let me help you,' he said, and wiped up the coffee she had slopped into the saucers before he perched on a stool opposite her at the breakfast bar.

Her eyes drank him in: the unruly brown hair, the red tinge visible with the sunlight streaming on it from the window behind him; the strong-featured face with its mobile mouth; the penetrating eyes, hooded by heavy lids that gave him a saturnine expression that changed when he smiled. There was nothing about him she disliked, except perhaps his clothes. But that was a question of money, not taste.

'Stop looking at me so soulfully,' he ordered. 'What I said to you last night still stands.'

'You mean you can just leave me? Be happy never to see me again?'

'It's better for both of us if I do.' He drained his coffee and rose.

'My parents want me to go to America for three months, maybe longer,' she said in a rush.

Her words stopped him in his tracks, though his face showed no emotion. 'I'm sure you'll enjoy yourself there.'

'I know I will.' She leaned back and clasped her hands behind her head, aware that the movement accentuated her breasts, and experiencing a thrill of triumph when she saw his eyes involuntarily drop to them and linger.

'When are you leaving?' he asked huskily.

'Soon. Will you mind?'

'I can't afford to.'

'That wasn't what I asked.' She dropped her hands and leaned towards him, her thick golden hair swinging provocatively forward. 'Will you miss me?'

'You know bloody well I will!'

'I haven't said I'll go yet.'

His hands clenched so tightly at his sides that the muscles on his arms bulged. 'What do you want me to do, Diana? Beg you to stay?'

'Just ask, that will be enough.'

'I can't ask. I've nothing to offer you.'

'You have yourself. That's all I want.'

'Do you honestly think your parents will be happy for you to go on seeing me?'

'I have my own life to live,' she cried, ignoring his question. 'And when Daddy knows how much you mean to me, he'll be more than willing to help you.'

'I'd never accept help from your father. Haven't you learned anything about me?' Adam flexed his hands in front of her. 'These have given me my independence, and one day this——' he tapped his temple '—will make my fortune. *My* fortune, sweetheart, made with *my* hands and *my* brain. Not a bank account filled by someone's Daddy!'

His reaction was understandable and Diana could have kicked herself. Why on earth had she been so tactless? She blamed it on desperation, but unless she managed to repair the damage, he would walk out on her.

'I'm sorry,' she apologised in a small voice. 'It's just that I love you so much, I can't bear for us to part.' She allowed the tears she had been holding back to surface, aware that few men were able to resist a woman crying, and praying Adam was no exception. 'Please, darling, say you forgive me.'

His features softened, the anger disappearing as he stepped around the bar, and drew her to her feet.

'It seems as if you're always apologising, and I'm always forgiving,' he muttered. 'But it doesn't change anything, Di. We're in an impossible situation.'

'Nothing's impossible if you want me enough. And you do want me, don't you?'

Moisture-filled eyes, luminous as bluebells in the morning dew, met warm brown ones, and his resistance visibly crumbled. With a groan he gathered her close, raining tiny kisses on her eyelids, the curve of her cheek, the corners of her mouth.

'This is all wrong,' he whispered, but the trembling of his body belied his words, as did the heat of his mouth as it covered hers. It moved over her lips as if he wished to devour her, his tongue rubbing against hers as if to absorb her into his very being.

Diana pressed herself tightly to him, revelling in the hard feel of his muscles, the firm touch of his hands on her breasts, her hips. Deeply she breathed in the smell of him, the warmth of his breath, the moisture of his skin. He meant everything to her. He was her life, her world.

She was aware of being lifted off her feet, and she clasped her arms round his neck as he strode to the bedroom. Gently he placed her on the bed and lay down beside her, his hands expertly undoing the buttons of her dress until the material gave way and her breasts were exposed. Only then did he draw away, his eyes softening as they took in her naked loveliness. With a groan he lowered his head and took a nipple in his mouth, sucking it hard. Diana was swept by wave upon wave of passion, and unaware of Adam removing the rest of her clothes, and discarding his, until he was suddenly naked beside her, his sinewy body pressing upon her soft flesh.

With a murmur she nestled close, curve against curve, and he began caressing her, his mouth following his fingers as they stroked her pointed breasts until they swelled and hardened, then moved down the gentle swell of her stomach to the downy triangle below it. At the feel of the soft hair he groaned deep in his throat, and with the tip of his tongue licked the very heart of her, sucking the pulsating nub until she cried with ecstasy and twined her legs around his.

No man had touched Diana with such intimacy, and she was alight with passion, burning with a desire she had never before experienced. Tentatively she touched his manhood, nervously stopping as it leapt beneath her hand. Then she touched it again, rubbing her hand up and down the length of it and feeling it grow larger and harder. Fiercely she pulled him closer still, encompassing him with her legs and pressing her moist, downy triangle of hair upon the springing muscle. She wanted Adam inside her, wanted him to possess her and make her his.

Holding him tightly, she turned on to her back and pulled him with her. For an instant he resisted, then with an anguished cry he mounted her and instantly plunged into the hot, moist darkness. A flash of pain pierced her, but even as she cried out, it was overwhelmed by the greatest sensation of pleasure she had ever known. Hands upon his buttocks, she urged him to push deeper into her, revelling in the jutting spear of flesh that pounded and reared inside her. As one they rose and fell, and as the engorged swell of him expanded and filled her, she moved faster and faster.

'I love you,' she cried against his lips. 'Say you love *me*.'

'I do, I do,' he said thickly, and thrust upwards so hard and deep that she felt he was penetrating her womb.

His movements intensified and she clung to him, her body rocking with his urgent possession as passion became her master and she spiralled towards another dimension. Repeatedly he plunged into her, carrying her with him to a shuddering, towering climax that had her screaming her release into his sweat-streaked skin.

They must have drifted off to sleep, for when Diana awoke, the brilliant golden sunlight had faded to a rosy haze. Turning her head she saw Adam watching her, his eyes shadowed by a thick strand of hair that had fallen across his forehead.

'You're beautiful,' he said gruffly. 'Even more beautiful now than before.'

'Do I look different, then?' she asked with a shy smile.

'Completely!'

'I feel wonderful.' She rested her head upon his shoulder. 'You're a wonderful lover, Adam. Was it— was it good for you?'

He appeared amused by her uncertainty. 'What do you think?'

'I can't judge. It was the first time for me.'

'I know.' A sigh came from deep within him, and she was aware that the knowledge didn't please him.

'Was it so obvious?' she questioned anxiously, pulling back to look at his face.

'That wasn't why I sighed,' he answered.

'Then why?'

'Because I didn't want to be the first. If I'd had any idea you were a virgin...'

'I'm glad I was. I wanted you to be the first.'

'I should never have taken advantage of you. I should have been stronger.'

'You didn't take advantage of me. I wanted you as much as you wanted me.'

'I shouldn't have given in,' he insisted. 'I must have been crazy.' He stopped abruptly as he saw her lips tremble. 'Don't cry, please don't.' His voice held a depth of emotion that surprised her, and her tears fell faster.

'Di, don't. I didn't mean to upset you. I only...'

With an exclamation he pulled her close, then rolled her on to her back and straddled her. His mouth stifled her sobs, and the hard line of his cheek rubbed away her tears as, with desperate urgency, he pushed her legs apart and entered her again.

She was not ready for him and because of it felt him the more; aware of the thick bulging muscle inside her, a heavy fullness of flesh moving in and out, slowly arousing her. But this was a deeper arousal than before as his finger flicked between her slender thighs, seeking and finding the precise spot that would awaken new sensations, send her to new heights of passion. Gently he

caressed the hot tender flesh and she cried out in won-
drous joy. Only then did he give way to his own pleasure,
bursting into her with such force that he carried her with
him again to a quivering, shattering climax that left them
damp and panting.

'Marry me,' she whispered, hardly knowing what she
was saying until she heard herself. Only then did she
realise she wanted it more than anything else in the world,
and she clasped her arms round his neck and stroked
the damp skin.

'Marry me,' she whispered again.

Slowly he lifted himself off her and sat up. 'This hasn't
changed anything,' he said flatly. 'Today was a one-off,
not a prelude to marriage.'

'But you love me—you've just proved it.'

'All I've proved is that I'm not as strong as I thought
I was. I knew what you were angling for when you asked
me here.'

'You didn't take much persuading,' she answered
harshly.

'That cuts both ways.' Reaching down to the floor, he
picked up his jeans and slipped into them. 'Chalk me
up to experience. A month from now you'll be laughing
about me with your girlfriends.'

'That's a horrid thing to say!'

'The truth is often cruel.' He shrugged into his T-shirt.
'I can't afford you, Diana, and not just for financial
reasons.'

'You mean I'd be a drag,' she said bitterly.

'If you want me to be blunt—yes. I have to make my
own way, and I can do that best if I don't have any
emotional attachments. So don't try to see me again. It
won't work a second time.'

Only as the front door closed behind him did Diana
give full vent to her hurt and anger. Jumping out of bed,
she stamped around the room, damning Adam for his

ambition, his ability to walk away from her, but mostly for his stupid pride. Why was it wrong to let her father help him when he had finished his studies? Why insist on going it alone if it meant never seeing her again? So much for his professed love!

Blinking away her tears, she went to the bathroom to shower. She was crazy to have bothered with him in the first place. He was happy in his dreary little world and that was exactly where he deserved to be.

Even as she thought this, she knew she didn't mean it. There was something about Adam that touched her as no other man had. It wasn't just physical either; it was the way he thought, the things he believed in. Yes, the very things that had made him walk out on her.

Returning to the bedroom to dress, she saw the rumpled sheet where they had lain. Gathering it close, she breathed in the fragrance of their lovemaking, acknowledging that she would do anything in the world to live her life with him.

'I won't let you escape me,' she said aloud. 'I'll give you a few days to cool off and then I'll go to see you.'

With renewed vigour she remade the bed with fresh sheets, stowed the used ones in the laundry basket and left the apartment, vowing that by hook or by crook she would become Adam's wife.

CHAPTER SEVEN

It was four weeks before Diana admitted that Adam meant what he had said when he had walked out of Hugo's apartment. She had tried everything she could think of to make him change his mind; pestered him at the garage until he had warned her he might lose his job, waited for him outside the polytechnic at night, to beg him to continue seeing her as a friend and not a lover; anything rather than cutting her out of his life.

But to no avail. He could have been made of steel, so hard and unbending was he, so firm in his belief that to see her would result in misery for them both.

'It will be years before I'm in a position to marry anyone—let alone a girl like you,' he had reiterated the last time she had seen him, when he had reluctantly agreed to come into her car and talk to her. 'Forget me, and find someone in your own world.'

'I don't want anyone else. It's *you* I love! You're cruel to let money stand between us. Why won't you let my parents help you until you've established yourself? Don't go!' she had cried, as he went to open the door.

'Then stop shoving your parents' money at me. I don't want their help. How often do I have to tell you?'

'Then take mine instead. I'll get a full-time job and pay my own way. I won't be a burden, Adam, I promise.'

He slammed out of the car, then bent to speak to her through the half-open window. 'You don't begin to know what makes me tick, do you? Don't come looking for me again, Diana. If you do, I'll walk right past you.'

Driving home with tears of frustration pouring down her cheeks, she had finally accepted he meant what he said, and in the ensuing weeks she had flung herself into a hectic social round of parties and country weekends.

Yet he still haunted her dreams. Night after night she awoke crying for him, at the same time furious that he had the emotional strength to walk out of her life.

Gradually the long days of summer were superseded by the shorter ones of autumn, but Diana was no nearer forgetting Adam than when they had parted two months earlier.

'I wish you'd go and stay with Aunt Leona,' her mother said one afternoon in mid-September. 'Virginia's beautiful at this time of the year, and you'd have a wonderful time.'

'I'm having a great time here,' Diana retorted. 'David's on the verge of asking me to marry him, and Julian wants me to be his live-in girlfriend.'

'I hope you'll say no to both.'

Diana's lovely eyes, overly large in a face that had thinned considerably these past weeks, regarded her mother mockingly. 'I imagined you'd approve of David. He's heir to a title.'

'He's also forty and drinks too much.' Her mother's tone dripped acid. 'Don't throw your life away out of pique because your father and I didn't approve of Adam. I know you aren't seeing him, but it's perfectly obvious you haven't forgotten him.'

'I never will!'

'Don't be foolish. In six months you won't remember what he looks like.'

'You couldn't be more wrong!'

Banging the door behind her, Diana stormed upstairs and flung herself on her bed, though she immediately regretted her childish behaviour. Arguing over Adam served no purpose other to annoy her mother. She would apologise, and suggest they went to Fortnum's for tea; they both adored the cream pastries that were served there. Yet the idea of food nauseated her. Come to think of it, she had felt off colour the whole week. Perhaps she was sickening for something. Maybe that's why her period was late.

Slowly a dreadful conviction dawned, and she ran to look at herself in the full-length mirror in her bathroom. She did not appear any different, but then why should she? Her scalp prickled and she stood rooted to the spot, so panic-stricken that her surroundings swirled giddily. In her mad, crazy longing for Adam, she hadn't given a thought to taking precautions.

Collecting her purse, she quietly left the house and made for the nearest chemist, where she bought a pregnancy testing kit. She returned home with it, feeling as guilty as if she were carrying heroin and, in the solitude of her bathroom did the test.

No doubt about it. She was pregnant.

Expecting her panic to intensify, she was amazed to find it had miraculously receded, leaving her with a deep sense of exaltation. Adam couldn't refuse to see her now!

With the best part of a day to kill, she occupied herself by debating how to play her forthcoming meeting with him. One thing was positive. The baby was her key card and she intended using it to her full advantage.

Deciding the best way to catch Adam was when he was leaving college, she arrived just before nine o'clock. Parking her car in a side turning, she hurried to the entrance.

She saw him before he saw her, and her heart thumped painfully in her chest at sight of his swinging walk, head held high as if challenging the world. How handsome he was, and how unaware of it as he came down the steps, past a group of girls who eyed him with interest. Only as he reached the last step did he see Diana, and his foot faltered before he turned sharply and walked rapidly away from her.

Startled, for she had at least expected him to stop and say hello, she called his name and raced after him. As if he did not hear, he went on walking.

'Adam,' she panted, 'I have to talk to you.'

'Don't you ever give up?' he bit out, increasing his pace.

'I wasn't going to bother you again, but I've something important to tell you.'

'What is it?'

She tried to speak but couldn't. Tension was having its effect on her and she felt giddy and light-headed. 'Do stand still a minute,' she cried irritably. 'I don't feel well.'

This brought him to a stop, though his expression was suspicious as he surveyed her. Close to him, she noticed his face had grown thinner, the cheekbones protruding from the tightly stretched skin, the jaw more pugnacious. Despite the indifference he pretended, she saw that their parting had distressed him as much as it had her.

'I'm waiting,' he said.

She tried to speak but her mouth was so dry that all her carefully rehearsed words refused to come out.

Misinterpreting her silence, he frowned. 'You shouldn't have come out if you're ill.'

'I'm not ill.' She stopped. 'Adam, I——'

'Let's have a drink,' he cut in abruptly, and headed for the café on the corner. It was half empty, and with a nod he indicated a table by the window, then went over to the counter.

From her seat, Diana watched him, taking in the straight back, the erectly held head with its thatch of thick, unruly hair. As he paid for the coffee and turned towards her, the light from an overhead lamp shone on him and she caught a glint of dark red. Then he was beside her, setting the cup in front of her with a work-roughened hand.

Silently he took the chair opposite but made no move to touch his cup. His expression was sombre, his sherry-brown eyes lifeless, and she had the intuitive feeling he was forcing himself to eschew all emotion.

'I'm pregnant,' she said into the silence.

'*You're what?*'

'I'm going to have your baby.'

'Oh, God!' This time his anguish was apparent. 'I never thought... I assumed you... Are you sure?'

'Yes. I had a test this morning.' Diana was close to tears. Although she had not expected him to be over-joyed at her news, she had naïvely hoped he would show a caring concern for her. But it seemed she was wrong; his concern was for himself.

'What a mess!' he muttered, banging his hand so hard on the table that the cups clattered. 'This is all I need!'

Scared, she half rose, and he reached out and gently pushed her down again.

'I'm sorry,' he said thickly. 'I didn't mean to frighten you. It's just that I could kick myself for not taking precautions.' He rubbed his hand across his cheek. 'Tell me when, and I'll come with you.'

'If you mean what I think you mean, then it's no. I intend having our child.'

'You're crazy!' Only now did his eyes come alive, gleaming like jet in a face white with shock.

'Don't misunderstand me,' she said lightly. 'I'm not asking you to marry me, nor do I require maintenance.' The scene was proceeding as she had anticipated, and her hours of rehearsal were paying off. 'I haven't for-gotten all the plans you've made for your future and I wouldn't dream of standing in your way. I only told you I'm pregnant because you're the father and I felt you

had a right to know. You may want to see it one day
and——'

'*Shut up!*' Adam's voice was so loud that several
people turned to regard them. 'Is that what you think
of me? That I'd let you have my child and not marry
you?'

'It's not unusual to be a single parent these days, and
I can afford help.'

'A father is more important to a child than money. *I*
should know that if anyone does! We're getting married
and that's the end of it.'

The raw pain in his voice hurt her, and never had she
loved him more. 'I feel so guilty, Adam.'

'It was my fault as much as yours.' He sighed heavily.
'What did your parents say?'

'I haven't told them. I wanted you to be the first to
know.'

This was only partly true. Aware that her parents
would urge her to have an abortion, and of the rows that
would ensue when she refused, she had decided not to
tell them until she and Adam were safely married, though
how she was going to accomplish this she had not yet
worked out.

'I hope they won't believe I made you pregnant deliberately?' he muttered.

'Knowing how I feel about you, they might assume it
was the other way round!'

'Would they be right?'

'No. To be honest, it didn't enter my head. But I'd
be lying if I said I'm sorry it's happened. I'm glad I'm
carrying your child.'

As if against his will, he half smiled. 'You're so
damned ingenuous!'

She remained silent and he reached for her hand. 'Your
folks may feel I'm a fortune-hunter, but when they see
I intend for us to live on what *I* earn, I hope they'll

change their opinion. I can only give you the necessities, Di, but we won't starve.'

'Budget menus will probably be better for the baby,' she giggled.

'I'm not sure how my landlady will take to the idea of a screaming child,' Adam said uneasily. 'You haven't been to my place, have you?'

Diana shook her head. He had never offered to take her there, and guessing it to be far from salubrious, she had not suggested it. 'Why don't we go now?' she ventured. 'Is it near here?'

'In Kilburn. Not a district you'll like.'

She understood why when, following his directions, she drew her car to a stop outside a tall, dingy terraced house in an equally dingy street off Kilburn High Road. She was thankful it was dark, and that there weren't many people around, for her red Mercedes was embarrassingly conspicuous among the cheap cars and motorbikes of the other residents.

The hallway of the house was narrow and dank and smelled of over-cooked cabbage, and her heart sank. It sank further when they reached the fourth floor and he opened the door to his bedsitter. She had not expected much, but this was worse than she had imagined.

The entire area was smaller than her bedroom, and contained a small wooden table and two chairs, a brown, well-worn imitation leather couch, a small hi-fi system with a fair-sized collection of discs and tapes on the table beside it, and in the far corner, a wood dais covered by a double mattress and duvet. Not even a proper bed, she saw with horror.

'Not what you're used to, is it?' he stated glumly.

'I don't care as long as we're together.' She glanced at the table. 'I'm glad it's not big enough for dinner parties. I'm a rotten cook!'

'We can't afford them anyway. Fancy another coffee?'

'I'd love one,' she lied, wanting to occupy him while she looked round to see how she could improve the room. Whatever he said to the contrary, she was convinced that once they were married he would allow her to spend her own money on refurbishment. A few kitchen units could replace the open shelves on the wall, and a coloured enamel sink could replace the mottled china one. A microwave and combination grill would fit on the draining board, while a proper bed with frilly bed linen was essential.

The only good thing that could be said for the room in its present state, was that it was spotless; the worn carpet, whose pattern was indiscernible, was dust free, and the navy and white patterned duvet cover and pillow cases appeared freshly laundered. Diana was not surprised at this. Adam's clothes might be cheap, but other than when he was at work, they were always immaculately clean, as he was himself.

'You make good coffee,' she praised, as she sipped from the mug he had handed her.

'It's the cheapest instant you can buy.'

'Goes to show what a waste of money the dearer ones are!'

'You'll be telling me next you'd rather live here than in Knightsbridge,' he said flatly.

'I would, if it's with you.'

'You really mean that, don't you?'

'I wouldn't be here if I didn't. I wasn't expecting a palace.'

'Then you haven't been disappointed!'

With relief Diana saw his face lighten with humour. Perhaps the worst was over.

'I'd better be going,' she said, noticing how late it was. 'I'd like to spend a penny first.' She glanced round. 'Which door is the bathroom?'

'I don't have one of my own. I share it with three other tenants.'

It was an effort for Diana to hide her horror, and she said a silent prayer that she had turned away to collect her purse when Adam answered. But when she saw the bathroom she was relieved to find it clean and tidy, with an instant immersion heater, a small bath, and a spartan shower cubicle.

It was no worse than her boarding-school, she thought as she drove home shortly afterwards, and would be quite bearable for a few months. She was certain she wouldn't have to live there longer than that. When she was Adam's wife she stood a better chance of making him see reason where finances were concerned.

She had arranged to meet him next day to discuss the wedding arrangements, but they had already agreed it should be a quiet one at a register office.

'I'd feel like a fish out of water if you wanted a big "do",' he had said.

'I don't. Besides, it would take months to arrange and—and——'

'You don't fancy walking up the aisle noticeably pregnant!'

'Right.'

'Poor Di. I've done you out of a day to remember, haven't I?'

'I only need *you* there to make it a day to remember,' she had cried, cuddling close to him and wondering what he would say when he learned she wasn't going to tell her parents about their marriage until the knot was tied. He was so honest, she doubted he would agree to it, and indeed she was already having second thoughts. Perhaps if Adam was with her when she told them about the baby, they might not be so judgemental. She would re-consider the position tomorrow, when she was feeling more clear-headed.

But fate decided for her. When she came downstairs in the morning, one look at her father informed her something was wrong.

'Is it Mother?' she asked.

'Yes. Her depression is back.'

'How bad is it?'

'She'll have to go into the nursing home. She's completely withdrawn. I'm taking her there this morning.'

'I'll come with you,' Diana said at once, and grabbing a piece of toast, ran up to see her mother.

It was a sad and silent journey to Surrey, and an even sadder return, for the resident psychiatrist, who knew her mother well, had said it would probably be some weeks before she had recovered sufficiently to return home.

'Why don't you take a holiday?' her father suggested as they entered the house. 'It's pointless visiting your mother when she's like this, and she'd prefer you to go away.'

In the hope that it will make me forget Adam, Diana realised. 'I might go somewhere with Jane,' she murmured, confident her friend would back her lie.

'Good. On Friday I'm off to Japan for a week, and I'd be happier if we were both away at the same time.'

This fitted in perfectly with Diana's plans, and the wedding was arranged for the day after her father's departure. She had explained the nature of her mother's illness to Adam, saying that because of it she was loath to upset her father further by telling him of her pregnancy and marriage.

'Do you think it's fair to keep him in the dark?' Adam questioned. 'He'll be very hurt, and angry too.'

'He'll understand why I did it,' she replied. 'And when the baby comes it will all be forgotten.'

So did Diana appease her conscience. When you wanted something badly enough it was easy to persuade yourself it was right, and as she drove to the register office, Jane at her side, her only thought was for Adam, and their future life together.

CHAPTER EIGHT

BANGING and shouting resounded in Diana's ears and she sat up sharply, aware of Adam pounding angrily on the next-door wall.

'I'll kill those bloody people,' he growled, his strong buttocks and thighs outlined by the street lights outside, which shone into their room. 'I've had enough of them.'

'They're not always as noisy as this,' she said quietly, hoping to defuse the situation. 'Forget it and come back to bed.'

'No. This is no place for you to live—to make love to you. It's bloody undignified!'

The pain in his voice told he saw it as a reflection on his manhood that he could not afford better. Yet he still refused to consider the alternative she had suggested.

'When my parents see how happy I am with you, they'll be delighted to buy us a flat. It needn't be an expensive one. Just——'

'No!' he had exploded. 'You're my wife and *I'll* take care of you.'

Recollecting this, she was silent as she flung aside the duvet and padded over to where he was disconsolately staring out of the window. She ran butterfly kisses along his shoulders and down his arms, then rested her face upon his back and brushed her mouth across it, gradually moving it down his spine till she reached the soft roundness of his buttocks. The angry tension of his muscles melted away, replaced by tension of a different kind.

With a groan he swung round and lifted her into his arms, striding across the small space to set her on the bed and come down on top of her.

'I love you,' she whispered into the heat of his mouth, her declaration sending him into a vortex of passion he could not control. It was often this way between them, their desire for each other so powerful that the tiniest spark set it off.

At weekends they frequently spent the entire day making love, finding new ways, new places, to arouse and please. Diana was amazed at the depth of her sexuality, and Adam's virility in keeping pace with her. A touch was enough to arouse her, and one look was sufficient to set her thighs quivering, aching for his hands and lips.

Thirty minutes later, as Adam lay sound asleep, Diana stared at the shadows on the wall. Later today she was going to tell her parents she was married. Her mother had returned from the nursing home yesterday, and Diana had spoken to her on the telephone, pretending she was still in the South of France with Jane.

She had hated lying to her parents, and these past weeks had been racked by guilt, but she was so deliriously fulfilled with Adam, she felt the end justified the means.

Too nervous to sleep, she was in the bathroom showering at six, careful to be as quiet as possible, then crept back to their room to sit by the window. At seven, dressed in a Paul Costelloe white jacket and navy linen trousers, she switched on the electric kettle and put two slices of bread in the toaster. It was old and the timer didn't work, and as usual she forgot to watch it.

'Luckily I love the smell of burnt toast!' Adam teased from the bed, stretching himself awake.

'I'll make some more,' she offered at once.

'Don't bother. Just scrape off the worst bits and put on plenty of butter and marmalade.'

She did so, then set the plate on the table. Adam padded across to join her, a towel wrapped round his middle. With a murmur he nuzzled the side of her neck.

'Hmm, you smell delicious. I think I'll eat *you* instead!'

'The way I feel this morning, you would be better off not to!'

'Poor darling. Still queasy?'

She nodded and broke off a piece of dry toast for herself. Her appetite had not completely returned, and mornings were the worst for nausea. It was quite normal, the gynaecologist at the hospital had assured her when she had gone for her first check-up, but that didn't make it easier to bear.

'I think I should go with you to see your parents,' Adam said. 'I feel guilty letting you face the music alone.'

'It will be easier on my own. If they see you with me it would be like a red rag to a bull.' Only as she saw a flush mount his cheeks did she realise her comment was less than flattering. 'Give them a chance to get used to the idea. Once they have, they'll grow to love you as much as I do.'

They were brave words, for she was far from convinced they were realistic.

'What will you do if they won't forgive you?' he asked. 'If they throw you out?'

'They'll never do that. Especially when they learn about the baby. It's my trump card.'

'They might still refuse to have anything to do with *me*.'

'Then I won't see them.'

Before he had a chance to comment, she switched on her hairdrier, unwilling to continue a conversation that was only increasing the butterflies in her stomach.

It was a relief when Adam left for the garage, and she mooched around the bedsitter for the best part of an hour before going to her car.

The nearer she drew to her parents' home, the more nervous she became. She loved them and would be devastated if they didn't forgive her. For the umpteenth time she debated how to break the news. Should she lead up to it or be blunt?

She was no nearer an answer when she entered the drawing-room and ran across to hug her mother. 'You look great,' she said happily.

'I feel it. I'm on some new pills.'

'What time did your plane get in?' her father enquired.

With a start Diana remembered she was supposed to have returned from the South of France this morning! Her heart pounded and she wished she had had the courage to be honest from the beginning. But it was too late for regrets. She was Adam's wife and they had to be told.

'I—er—I didn't go to France.'

'Didn't go? Where were you then?'

Clenching her hands, Diana launched into her story. Her parents listened in silence, and only when she said she was expecting a baby did her father give a strangled gasp.

'The swine! So that was how he caught you!'

'It wasn't like that at all. If you want the truth, *I* seduced *him*.'

'Diana, how could you?' her mother cried in anguish. 'He's so wrong for you, so different, so——'

'So poor. That's what you really mean. If he were rich you'd welcome him with open arms.'

'That isn't true. He's too blunt, too aggressive.'

'He's honest and determined,' Diana corrected. 'He's also ambitious and clever.'

'Clever enough to catch *you*,' her father said bitterly.

Her mother began to cry and helplessly Diana watched as her father went over to her and patted her shoulder. Gradually her mother's tears subsided, and only then did Mr Farrow turn to his daughter.

'You are a headstrong, foolish girl, but you've presented us with a situation we can't change, and we'll have to make the best of it.'

'Oh, Daddy, I'm so glad! I promise you won't regret it.' Diana flung herself into his arms, laughing and crying. 'When you know Adam better you'll love him. And he didn't marry me for my money. Knowing we were rich put him off.'

'Not for long,' her mother sniffed.

'I forced his hand,' Diana confessed, her cheeks rosy with embarrassment. 'But he insists that we live on what he earns.'

'Does he honestly believe we'd let you?' her father demanded. 'Until he has qualified and can earn a decent salary, he'll work for *me*.'

'I don't think he will.'

'We'll see. Have dinner with us tonight, but don't mention I'm going to offer him a job.'

'If he says no, don't argue with him, Daddy. Promise me?'

Her father patted her cheek. 'I promise. Just relax and let me deal with him my way.'

To Diana's relief the evening went off better than she had anticipated, apart from the initial few moments of stilted conversation. Her parents were determinedly friendly, and by the time they sat down to dinner, an onlooker would have considered them a normal, happy family.

The meal over, the two men went off to her father's study, ostensibly to look at his stamp collection. Diana tried to hide her nervousness, but though she kept a conversation going with her mother, she was alert to any sounds that might erupt from the room across the hall. All seemed quiet, but after half an hour she grew restless and was considering whether to go in and see what was happening, when the two men rejoined them.

The satisfied expression on her father's face, and the resigned one on Adam's, indicated that the matter had been resolved, though neither of them referred to it, and it was only as they drove home that Adam gave her some idea of what had occurred between him and his father-in-law.

'If you hadn't been pregnant, I'd have turned him down flat. But I won't take the chance of money worries affecting your health and the baby.'

'It will be marvellous not having to count the pennies any more,' Diana agreed. 'Now I can go to the supermarket and buy as many kiwis as I want! It's funny, but until I was pregnant, I didn't even like them.'

'I'm glad it's kiwis and not caviare you fancy,' Adam smiled. 'I'm not getting paid *that* much. Your father offered me a crazy amount but I refused to take more than I'm worth. It's the only way I can accept his help.'

But as the weeks passed it was apparent he was not finding it easy to work for her father.

'Had a bad day?' she asked one evening when he arrived home looking more troubled than usual.

'No worse than any other.'

'It has to be better than pumping petrol,' she couldn't help saying.

'Checking figures all day isn't stimulating either,' he replied sourly.

'It won't be for long, darling. Once you have your degree you'll be able to find something that interests you.'

Her reassuring words did not improve his mood, and she was dismayed when, at the end of the week, he informed her he had walked out.

'Your father may be easy at home, but at work he's a tyrant, and I told him so,' Adam informed her bluntly. 'I've managed to get my old job back, and they've also agreed to let me work from midnight till six three nights a week. So that will bring in extra cash.'

'You can't do that. You'll be exhausted.'

'Hard work won't kill me.'

Diana forced herself not to argue. Her father could be irascible, but Adam had the intelligence to cope with it, if he wanted. Trouble was, he didn't, and had taken the easy option. Except it wasn't going to be easy for *her*. Anger bubbled inside her. However much Adam disliked his job, he should have put up with it until he had qualified.

Her parents thought the same and made no bones about it, which did not improve their relationship with Adam. An uneasy peace prevailed whenever they saw each other, which fortunately wasn't too often, for his hours at the garage were long, and left little time to socialise. He was also studying hard, and as the strain began to tell on him, he grew increasingly short-tempered.

Yet nothing could spoil their joy of the child they were expecting, and when Diana experienced its first flutter he was as thrilled as she was.

'My clothes won't fit much longer,' she said, inspecting herself in the mirror, and noticing her thickening waist. 'Luckily the dress I'm wearing for Jane's party tonight was a bit loose when I bought it, otherwise I don't know what I'd do.'

Adam, his chestnut-brown eyes appraising the soft curves of her young breasts, suddenly looked uneasy.

'I'm afraid I can't go with you, Di. My tutor's offered me some extra tuition and I'm seeing him after college tonight.'

Dismay coursed through her. They rarely went anywhere together, and she had seen Jane's party as an opportunity to show off her handsome new husband to her friends.

'Can't you come on afterwards?' she suggested. 'It's Friday and the party's sure to go on till late.'

'I'll try.' His tone was so indifferent that she knew he wouldn't. 'If I don't make it, no one will miss me,' he went on. 'Your friends aren't mine, and never will be.'

'You haven't met any of them,' she accused. 'If you——'

'Let's not argue,' he cut in wearily. 'I'm not in the mood.'

Diana bit her lip to stop herself from saying he was never in the mood to discuss anything with her any more. Was it because he regretted being forced into their marriage, or was it the strain of having to study and do two jobs?

'I don't like you driving at night,' he commented as he rose to leave. 'Take a taxi there and back.'

Diana had intended to, apprehensive at returning late to the poorly lit street where they lived, and she ordered a mini-cab to collect her at eight o'clock.

When she arrived at Jane's home in Holland Park, the party was in full swing, and attempting to overcome her despondency she drank too much champagne. By midnight she had a raging headache, and was heading for the telephone to order a cab, when Jane's brother Hugo offered to take her home.

'Little sister insists,' he grinned. 'And so do I.'

'Thanks,' she smiled. 'You're both sweet.'

As his white Porsche drew up outside the peeling front door of the house in Kilburn, Diana was seeing it through his eyes, yet felt no shame. Rather she gloried in the knowledge that material things paled in comparison to being Adam's wife. They were going through a bad patch, but once he was qualified everything would be fine.

'I'll see you to your door,' Hugo insisted, and overruling her protest that it wasn't necessary, he escorted her up the four flights to the top of the house. 'Got your key?' he asked.

Diana searched her bag but couldn't find it. 'I must have left it in my other purse,' she giggled.

'No sweat. It's only midnight and your husband's sure to be waiting up for you.'

He pressed the bell and kept his finger on it until Diana reached out and laughingly pulled it away. She was still holding his hand when the door was flung open by Adam, a towelling robe concealing his naked body.

'Sorry, darling, did I wake you?' she asked, pulling Hugo forward. 'I'd like you to meet Hugo, Jane's brother. Wasn't it sweet of him to bring me home?'

'Very.' Unsmiling, Adam nodded in his direction. 'Sorry we can't ask you in, but as you see, I'm not dressed for entertaining.'

'Another time,' Hugo said easily, and tapping the tip of Diana's nose in farewell, loped down the stairs.

Diana waited till he was out of sight before going inside and closing the door. 'Oh, boy, do I have a headache.'

'I'm not surprised,' Adam snorted. 'You're drunk.'

'Merry,' she laughed. 'I missed you and had a third glass of champagne as compensation.'

'Wasn't that stupid twit compensation enough?'

'Hugo isn't stupid. He has a very successful estate agency.'

'Bought by Daddy, I suppose?'

'Do you always have to belittle everyone I know?' Diana exclaimed. 'Hugo's rich but his money didn't buy him a Double First at Cambridge. If you'd stop looking down your nose at my friends you might get to like them.'

'Pigs might fly!' Adam went towards the bed. 'You were a fool to marry me,' he called over his shoulder. 'You should have stuck with your own kind.'

Provoked, she lost her temper. 'I wish I had. I wish I'd had the sense to take the Pill!'

'Or have an abortion,' he added.

'You'd have liked that, wouldn't you? You suggested it the minute you learned I was pregnant. You never wanted this baby! That's why you've been so hateful to me. You resent being tied down.'

'Do you blame me? We were both stupid and irresponsible, and I've had to pay the price for it.'

'So have I.' Diana sank on to the nearest chair, shivering. The pain in her head was worse and she closed her eyes, opening them a moment later as Adam walked past her. He was in jeans and sweater, and shrugging into the suede jacket she had given him for his birthday.

'Where are you going?' she demanded.

For answer he slammed the door behind him.

What's happening to us? Diana thought fearfully, and, running to the door, she flung it open. 'Adam, come back!' she called, and rushed down the stairs after him.

The loose bit of carpet he had been promising to fix for weeks caught in one of her high heels. She flung out her arms to save herself, but her hand missed the banister, and with a scream she tumbled head first down the steep, narrow steps to the next landing.

CHAPTER NINE

DIANA heard someone calling her name and opened her eyes to see a figure in white bending over her. It was a nurse.

'Wh-where am I?' she asked fearfully. 'What's happened to me?'

'You had an accident,' the nurse said gently. 'You're in the Royal Free Hospital.'

'In hospital?' Diana's heart missed a beat as memory returned. 'My baby! Is it going to be all right?'

The sympathetic look on the woman's face was sufficient answer, and Diana burst into tears.

'It's upsetting, I know,' the nurse said, 'but you're young and healthy and you'll have other children.'

Diana wept harder, knowing she would never have another baby with Adam. He had not wanted this one, and had caused her to lose it. Not deliberately—she'd grant him that—but by default. If he had not walked out in anger...if he had nailed down the carpet as he had promised, instead of burying his head in those damned textbooks of his...

Ifs and buts chased round in her head, and when Adam walked into the ward some hours later she could hardly bear to look at him. He was carrying a bunch of flowers and placed them awkwardly on the coverlet.

'Forgive me, Di,' he muttered. 'I behaved like a swine. You can't say to me what I haven't already said to myself. But we'll have another baby...lots of them!'

'Will we?' she asked stonily.

'Of course. Maybe not yet, but later, when we can afford it.' He caught her hand and squeezed it. 'I know it's a great loss for you, but—but we love each other, and that's what counts.'

'Does it?' she questioned again, unmoved by his drawn features and words of remorse.

'Of course it does. I love you, Di.' He bent to kiss her and she recoiled from him as though he were a snake.

'I—I'll be back later,' he said jerkily, the hurt of her rejection registering on his face. 'You're still tired from the anaesthetic. By tomorrow you will see things differently.'

But as the days progressed and Diana recovered her strength, she still found it difficult to forgive Adam. In truth, she found it difficult to feel anything for him. Emotionally she was numb, and she responded to his loving overtures with a listlessness that worried him sufficiently to make an appointment for them to see one of the hospital's psychiatrists.

'A normal reaction,' he diagnosed after spending half an hour with them. 'Have a little patience, Mr Brooke, and your wife should soon be back to her old self.'

Because Diana showed little sign of this, and refused to leave their bedsitter, Adam finally agreed to let her recuperate at her parents' home, a request they had repeatedly made during the past month.

Adam refused to join her, though his father-in-law went out of his way to assure him he was more than welcome.

'I appreciate your invitation,' he said, 'but it will be easier for me if I stay in Kilburn. I'll come to see Di as often as I can, but living on my own will give me extra time to study.'

Naturally his studies came first, Diana thought bitterly. Until he achieved the success he dreamed of, she took second place in his life. Perhaps she always would.

'It's a long journey from Kilburn to here,' she said quietly. 'Don't put yourself out.'

'Adam can drive your car, Didi,' her father intervened.

'He's never driven my Mercedes, Daddy. It's against his principles to enjoy anything he didn't buy for himself.'

'I'm sure your father understands why,' Adam said tonelessly, heading for the door. 'Goodbye, Diana. I'll see you tomorrow.'

Diana settled into her old home as though she had never left it. The only difference was that she appreciated it more. What bliss to be back in her old room, with its dainty, hand-painted furniture, and matching curtains and blinds in Colefax and Fowler's 'Roses and Pansies' print of cream, red and green. The thick pile carpet was cream too, and her feet sank into it as she padded into the en-suite colour co-ordinated bathroom.

The thought of returning to the bedsitter she shared with Adam was appalling, and she shied away from it. Time enough to think of it when she was feeling better.

To her surprise, Adam came to see her every other day. He invariably came when her father was at business and her mother at one of her bridge games, and always found an excuse why he could not stay for a meal.

'Don't you *want* to see my parents?' she burst out on one occasion.

'Not particularly. They blame me for your miscarriage and——'

'Don't you?'

'You know I do. But facing their contempt, as well as my own remorse, is more than I can take right now.'

Appreciating the logic of this, Diana let the matter drop.

Within a few weeks she was more like her old self, and silently conceded that if their marriage were to continue, she and Adam had to compromise. She had no intention of going back to the old basis, where she was scared of accepting even a modicum of help from her father. She didn't expect to live in the lap of luxury, but nor did she think Adam should force her to live four flights up in a less than salubrious neighbourhood. But she would wait until they were living together again before broaching the subject.

On the very morning that Adam called to take her back to Kilburn, her father had a stroke and was rushed to hospital. Her mother, as always at times of stress, went to pieces, and Diana felt obliged to stay with her until her father recovered.

'Couldn't you at least come home at night?' Adam suggested. 'Your mother won't need you when she's asleep!'

'She often wakes up, even with sleeping pills, and I feel I should be here,' Diana replied.

She sympathised with Adam's resentment and the disruption her continued absence was having on his life but, worried that her mother's depression might return, she had no alternative.

'I miss you,' Adam muttered, drawing her close. 'It seems a lifetime since I held you in my arms.'

'You can stay here.'

'I'd rather not.'

None the less he went with her to the hospital as often as he could, and also made an effort to be nice to her mother, bringing her flowers and never disputing her most narrow-minded statements. So much so that she commented on it.

'Sometimes good does come out of tragedy, Adam. It's certainly changed *you*. You're becoming more like one of us every day.'

'Thank you, Mrs Farrow,' he answered gravely. 'I assume that's meant as a compliment.'

Fortunately the heavy irony was lost on her, though not on Diana.

Three weeks later, Mr Farrow was well enough to leave hospital, and Diana was free to return to her husband.

He called for her in the Mercedes—she knew better than to comment on it—and was teasing and affectionate. When he reached their front door he opened it, then swept her up into his arms.

'I never did carry you over the threshold.' His voice was low and throbbing. 'Welcome home, darling. I've missed you more than I believed possible.'

Their physical reunion was all she had hoped for, showing that in bed at least, nothing between them had changed. They barely made it to the mattress as, ripping off their clothes, they were consumed with a passion that knew no barriers. Diana was so wet there was no need for foreplay, and Adam plunged into her hard and strong as a battering ram, the climax brutal as they came together in violent, mindless, racking shudders.

Afterwards they lay exhausted upon the duvet, silently waiting for his manhood, which was still swollen inside her, to subside. But it quickly thickened and pulsated, and she moaned with the excruciating longing to have him take her again.

When he did, his lovemaking was leisurely, and he savoured her arousal, refusing her entreaties to plunge deeper and deeper.

'Not yet,' he whispered, rubbing his erect shaft backwards and forwards over the throbbing nub between her thighs, quieting his movements when she became too aroused, and slowly bringing her to such a fever of abandonment that she begged him to stay inside her.

Slowly he started rotating his hips, and movement for movement she matched him in perfect harmony. He grew wilder and so did she, clutching his strong buttocks, encouraging him to press harder and harder, higher and higher, until with a final thrust he burst inside her like a wildly gushing geyser, the liquid heat of him flooding through every fibre of her being.

She fell asleep in his arms, and awakened to the sight of his head on the pillow next to her—the thick brown hair tousled and still damp from their lovemaking. How young and vulnerable he looked, his features relaxed but still showing signs of tiredness and strain. Perhaps all would be well now, and they could make a fresh start; be as happy as they had been at the very beginning.

Unfortunately this was not to be, for the long hours he spent at the garage, followed by night school and studying at home, caused the tension between them to build up again. This time their quarrels were more acrimonious, fuelled by the emotional tug-of-war Diana was experiencing with her parents.

In spite of her father's continuing recovery, her mother was gradually lapsing into another depression, and Diana felt guilty if she didn't spend the best part of each day with them. She felt equally guilty for neglecting Adam, and tried her best to be home to prepare an evening meal for them.

Cooking had never been her forte, and she was so preoccupied with her parents that she started buying convenience foods in spite of the higher cost. To save even more time as she dashed from one side of London to the other, she bought a microwave, even though she knew Adam would be furious with her for accepting the money for it from her father.

'Other women manage on their husband's income,' he said angrily when he saw it. 'Why the hell can't you?'

'Because it isn't mandatory,' she answered wearily. 'I fail to see why I should suffer because of your stupid pride.'

'Where's the girl who was willing to give up everything providing we were together?' he sneered. 'It didn't take you long to miss Daddy's money.'

'For heaven's sake, he bought me a microwave, not a mansion!' Diana went to their tiny refrigerator and took out some packets of food. 'I have duck à l'orange, scallops in cream sauce, and salmon in a pastry case. What would you like?'

'A home-cooked meal,' he rasped, and striding over, slammed the fridge door shut, narrowly avoiding crushing her fingers in it as he did. 'If you insist on spending all your time with your parents instead of acting like a wife, at least have the sense to buy something filling, not this fancy rubbish. I'm a working man, not a jet setter!'

Seeing the clenched jaw, and the contempt in chestnut eyes that had once looked at her with love, she was nearer to hating him than ever before.

'Can't we have a simple argument without you turning it into a class war?' she cried.

Not waiting to hear his reply, she grabbed hold of her coat and rushed out, banging the door behind her.

As usual they made it up in bed, and for a few days peace reigned. However it was an uneasy one, and she knew it would take little to break it.

Returning to the bedsitter one evening, after a long and tiring day with her mother, she was touched to see the table set, and smell the appetising aroma of chicken roasting in the oven.

Adam was at the sink, draining vegetables, and he turned to smile at her. 'You've been looking so tired lately, I thought I'd make the dinner.'

Diana was amazed by his tenderness, so long absent from their relationship. 'That's very sweet of you. Thank you.'

'I should be thanking *you*,' he said huskily, striding over and gathering her close. 'Instead of appreciating what you went through to marry me, I've behaved like a boor.'

'No, you haven't.'

'Yes, I have. Don't argue with your husband!' His warm brown eyes glowed as they ranged over her face. 'I've decided we'll go away for Christmas. It will do us good to get away from all the pressures...to get to know each other again. I'll have to put in extra time at work to pay for it, but——'

'No, you won't.' Tears of joy sparkled in her eyes. 'I was going to tell you later, but as you've brought up the subject... Dr Lester thinks it would do my parents good to go on a cruise, and they'd like us to go with them. Just knowing I'm around will help Mummy cope. We won't have to spend much time with them,' she added hastily, as she felt his body tense against hers. 'Do say yes, darling,' she entreated. 'Being on board ship is so romantic, we can treat it as a delayed honeymoon.'

'How long will we be away?' he asked.

'Six weeks.'

'Six weeks? I can't get off for longer than ten days.'

'Why not? The polytechnic's closed for a month, and with Daddy paying for us we won't need the money from the garage.'

'It's not just a question of money. You know I've arranged to have extra tuition during the holidays, and I've no intention of cancelling it.'

'Can't you take your books with you and study in the cabin? Even if we were only together in the evenings it would be marvellous.' She looked up at him, her face alight with eagerness. 'Think of it, darling, six weeks of luxury with nothing to think about except each other.'

'And your parents,' he reminded her grimly, drawing away from her. 'You know how demanding your mother is. Anyway, why does she need you? Surely there are doctors and nurses on board?'

'They're strangers, and she needs the support of someone close.'

'So do I. Or don't I figure in your calculations?' His face was stiff with obstinacy. 'You have to make a choice, Diana. I won't go on the cruise, and if *you* do, then don't bother coming back to me.'

'You can't mean that!' she cried.

'I never say things I don't mean. You should know that by now.'

Horrified, she stared at him, seeing the tightly set mouth, the jutting chin, the determined stance.

'I can't let them down. Not after what Dr Lester said to me. If something awful happened while they were away, I'd never forgive myself. Can't you appreciate how I feel?'

'That's all I've done for months! What sort of life do you think it's been for me? You're hardly here, and when you are, you're too tired to do anything except sleep.'

'I'm never too tired to make love to you,' she retorted.

'There's more to marriage than sex.'

Diana caught her breath. Did Adam think she enjoyed playing nursemaid to a demanding mother? That she wasn't heart-broken to see her father struggling to get back to normal? Didn't he realise how torn she was between her love for her parents and her love for him? But Adam was young and healthy; too young and healthy to give her such an ultimatum. Hadn't he made her suffer enough by causing her to lose the baby? Surely he could put himself out just this once? Six weeks' holiday on board a luxury liner wasn't exactly purgatory!

'I want a wife.' He broke the silence. 'I realise you have divided loyalties, but you can't go on trying to cut yourself in two. You have to choose between us, Di. It's them or me.'

'You don't know what you're asking,' she said shakily. 'I love my parents and I love you. But there are occasions when one love takes precedence over another; as my love for you would take precedence if *you* were ill.'

'If the only way I can ever come first in your life is to be ill, then to hell with it!' he rasped. 'Make your choice. *Now.*'

Her throat contracted and she couldn't speak.

'Make your choice, Diana.'

Mutely she stared at him.

'You *have*, I take it,' he said harshly. 'And as expected, I'm the loser.' He walked swiftly to the door, then stopped and turned to her. 'I won't suggest *I* move out and you stay here,' he sneered. 'So I'll give you a couple of hours to pack. It shouldn't take you longer. Most of your clothes are still at Knightsbridge.'

'Adam, I——'

'No inquests,' he cut in. 'We've said it all. Enjoy your cruise, blondie. Without me, the rest of your life should be smooth sailing.'

The door closed behind him and the sound of his footsteps receded. Too bereft for tears, Diana sank into a chair and stared at the wall.

CHAPTER TEN

DIANA stood in her small, gloomy bedroom and slipped into her winter coat. It was a timeless Jaeger classic but the wrong length for this year's fashion; not surprising, considering it was six years old.

Six years. Hard to credit she and her mother had lived in this dreary flat for so long, and harder still to accept that from the moment she had packed her case and walked out of the bedsitter in Kilburn, she had never spoken to Adam; had no idea where he was or what he was doing.

She had tried to contact him from the cruise ship the night her father had died, and several times afterwards from Australia where, on the advice of the ship's doctor, her father had been buried to save her mother the strain of waiting for permission to fly the body back to England. But the telephone that served all the tenants in the house where they had lived had rung without answer, and the garage where Adam worked informed her he had left without giving a forwarding address.

In desperation she had contacted Jane, who had driven to Kilburn, seen that the house was boarded up and had a 'For Sale' sign outside it, and had then had the good sense to contact his college tutor. From him, Diana had finally learned that Adam had left London within days of their parting, and the tutor had never seen him again.

No one knew where he was, and Diana, coping with her mother's breakdown, which resulted in her spending two months in a Sydney nursing home, had no choice but to abandon the search.

Within days of their returning to London, she received a call from their family lawyer.

'Bad news, I regret to say. Glen Marrowvale, your late father's partner, shot himself last night.'

At first, she had not appreciated what impact this was going to have on their lives, but she soon discovered that the man had ruined the firm by disastrous investments in the stock market and, under a complicated agreement, her father's estate was responsible for the debts.

The house and contents had to go, and there was only enough left to put towards a tiny two-bedroom apartment in Camberwell, and put a thousand pounds on deposit in the bank, in case of emergencies.

Soon after they had moved in, their lawyer contacted Diana again to advise her that Adam had served divorce papers on her. It had been the final blow.

She had tried to contact him through the small legal firm who were representing him, hoping against hope for a reconciliation, but he had left strict instructions that he wanted nothing to do with her.

'I wish you didn't have to go out, Diana.'

Her mother's plaintive voice brought her back to the present, and she bit back a sigh. 'You know I have to work, darling. It's only for three hours, and there's a lovely old Paul Newman film on TV. By the time it's over I'll be back to prepare lunch.'

'Why won't you let *me* do the cooking? I'm not a child.'

'I don't want you overdoing things.' Diana was terrified her mother would leave a pan burning on the cooker and the whole apartment would go up in flames. Her arms around the bony shoulders, she led her into the sitting-room and settled her in front of the television.

'I dislike being left alone,' her mother said fretfully.

'I'll buy you the new *Harper's* today,' Diana placated, though she could ill afford it.

Lacking a degree or a skill, she had taken a job as a daily. It barely kept their heads above water, but it enabled her to return home at lunchtime, and to take time off if her mother was unwell, which was frequently the case.

Diana had long ago given up feeling sorry for herself, or thinking of the past when there had been no shortage of money. There were people worse off than herself, and she was thankful she did not have to ask for help from any of the Social Services.

Yet in spite of her positive attitude there were moments when she was near despair. Not because of their straitened circumstances, but the helplessness she felt at her mother's gradual decline into melancholia. And overlaying everything was the memory of Adam, which in the dark recesses of the night often returned to haunt her and make her long for him. But the best way to kill her desire for him was to remind herself how callously he had forced her to choose between her parents' genuine need of her and his purely selfish one.

Stepping off the bus outside Harrods—her beautiful Mercedes had long since gone, and the dilapidated old Renault Aunt Madge, her mother's sister, had given her was used only for special occasions—Diana walked down Walton Street to her first job of the day. Her employers were American; relaxed and informal enough for her to be on first-name terms with them. They were both in banking and she was more or less her own boss. The same applied to her afternoon job with Australians in Belgravia.

Both families entertained frequently, and she would often be asked to help them in the evening. This had taught her to cook, for she had assiduously watched the professional chefs who were always engaged for their parties. She could not afford to use the same expensive ingredients they did, but she skilfully adapted their recipes and obtained surprisingly similar results. Now, part of her weekends at home were spent in the kitchen, preparing meals for the following week. It was a relief from the television, which was never switched off. If she attempted to go to her bedroom to read, her mother followed her and insisted they talk.

'I spend my days alone, so the least you can do is to keep me company,' was her favourite complaint.

One of their few visitors was Aunt Madge, whose offer of financial help had been so grudgingly made that Diana had refused it, preferring independence to indebtedness. Mrs Farrow's friends had vanished long ago, not only because they were embarrassed by the difference in their lifestyles, but because of her withdrawal from reality.

'You ought to apply to the council for a home help,' Dr Lester advised one Saturday when he came to see them. Although they were no longer living in his area, he visited them every month.

'What good is a home help?' Diana questioned. 'They come twice a week and flick a duster.'

'It would save you doing it, and they'd also shop for you.'

Diana shook her head. Living on a tight budget, it was best to do her own shopping.

'You're a difficult girl to help,' Dr Lester commented as she saw him to his car. 'But you can't continue living a twilight life. You're only twenty-five, my dear. You should get someone to sit with your mother two or three evenings a week so you can go out. I remember you used to have a host of friends.'

He saw the answer in the tight set of her face, and gave a rueful sigh. 'I hope it isn't your pride that's keeping them away? A few of your friends may have turned out to be fair-weather ones, but I'm sure most of them would welcome you with open arms.'

'I'll think about it,' Diana lied. She had no desire to be an object of pity, which was what she would be if she tried to mix in her old circle again.

Yet in one respect the good doctor was right. Unless she took herself in hand, life would pass her by. She would find a sitter for her mother and enrol in evening classes to learn typing and word processing. They were skills that might provide the opportunity to get a better paid job.

Remembering the long hours Adam had worked and studied, she realised how vapid she must have seemed to him. A pity her parents had not inculcated some sense of responsibility into her, instead of regarding marriage to a rich young man as her only goal.

Her marriage to Adam had put paid to that notion, and even had the idea appealed to her now, her changed circumstances ruled it out. She had to build a future for herself and stop using her mother's ill health as an excuse to opt out.

Next morning there was an unusual bounciness in her step as she went to work. Passing a bus stop, she glimpsed an auburn-haired girl leaning close to a pleasant-looking man. They were obviously lost in their private world, and her thoughts flew back to her early halcyon days with Adam. She had believed their love could conquer everything, and that given time he would adapt to her way of life. No wonder she had lost him.

She had wounded his pride, and to a man like Adam, pride was important. Instead of appreciating his desire for independence, she had considered him selfish for wanting to drag her down to his level, not realising in her youthful stupidity that his level was way above hers. Had she been more understanding of his problems he might have been less condemnatory of her and her parents.

Yet he was not entirely blameless. His jealousy and temper had contributed to the accident that had lost her the baby, and his harsh ultimatum over the cruise had caused the break-up of their marriage.

The freshly painted façade of her employer's house came into view and Diana pushed away the past and opened the front door. As she did, the phone rang and she rushed to answer it. It was Jane.

'I called you at home but you'd just left,' her friend said. 'I haven't seen you for ages and I miss you. How about coming over on Saturday? A few of the gang are dropping in and they'd love to see you.'

'I already have a date,' Diana lied.

'Bring him with you. It *is* a him, I hope?'

'Yes, but we're going to a concert.'

'Join us afterwards.'

'If he hasn't planned anything else.'

'If you can't make it, meet me for lunch at Morton's next week.'

Knowing Jane would insist on paying—she always did—pride forced Diana to find an excuse.

'I'm working through my lunch-hours next week,' she lied again. 'But I'll call you the week after.'

'If not, I'll call *you*,' Jane replied. 'You've been fobbing me off for weeks, and I'm not letting you get away with it any longer.'

Jane had proved herself a true friend, and Diana felt guilty as she replaced the receiver. Trouble was, they no longer had much in common. In the past their main topics of conversation had been clothes, holidays and the latest fashionable restaurants. But these held only academic interest for her now; and while Jane also worked, it was still in her brother's estate agency, where she seemed able to come and go as she pleased.

Perhaps I'm too sensitive, Diana mused. I'm crazy to worry because I can't afford Jane's lifestyle. It's affection and loyalty that matters, and Jane has that in abundance.

Without further thought she dialled her friend's number. 'I made a mistake, Jane. My date is for Saturday week, so I'm free to come over.'

In unusual high spirits, she went into the kitchen to start on the ironing, her main Wednesday task. She was halfway through it when the telephone rang again. This time it was a nurse from King's College Hospital.

'Miss Farrow?'

'Yes.' Diana clutched the receiver. 'Is it my mother?'

'I'm afraid so. She had a stroke and your downstairs neighbour heard her fall and called the police.'

'How bad is she?'

'I think you'd better come at once.'

Sensing that her mother was dying, Diana left a note for her employer and took a cab to the hospital. The instant she saw the face of the young house doctor who greeted her at the entrance to the ward, she knew she had arrived too late.

'She didn't recover consciousness,' he murmured. 'So even if you had been with her, she wouldn't have known you.'

It was a small comfort, and blinking back her tears Diana sat by her mother's bed and clutched the frail hand until a kindly nurse led her away. She found it impossible to cry. How could she shed tears for a woman who had longed to die and join her husband? You're happy now, Mummy, she said silently. I just wish we'd been able to talk to each other properly before you finally left me.

'Do you have anyone to help you with the funeral arrangements?' the nurse asked.

'No. I have some relatives but I would rather do it myself.'

She had to inform Aunt Madge, of course, who would descend on her with Angela and Mark. She shivered, and decided to delay calling them until this evening. With luck they might be out at some function or other and not be able to come over till morning.

Late into the night Diana sat up, grateful that the few other members of the family and former friends with whom there remained some contact would not be with her till next day. She needed to be alone; it had become part of her persona.

'I've nothing more to lose,' she whispered, looking round the silent, empty room. 'I've learned to be strong and I can cope alone.'

CHAPTER ELEVEN

THE death of her mother left Diana with a sense of loneliness that hit her with full force in the weeks following the funeral. Her face grew gaunt and her high cheekbones finely etched, setting off blue eyes still luminous below a golden, but lank mane of hair.

'If you get any thinner, a puff of wind will blow you away!' Jane complained one evening when she dropped in unexpectedly. 'Why don't you take a few weeks off and we'll go to Italy? My treat, of course.'

'Thanks, but no.'

'You and your false pride. If——'

'It has nothing to do with pride,' Diana interrupted. 'It's just that I have too many things on my mind.'

'Such as?'

'I'll tell you when I've made my decision.'

'No, you won't. You'll tell me now so I can give you my opinion! Come on, spill the beans.'

'Well, I'm considering spending my savings on a computer cum business course, and then opening a domestic agency. My employers' friends are always asking if I know anyone for them, or trying to poach *me*, so there's obviously a demand.'

'There are also hundreds of agencies.'

'I know. But I intend specialising in bachelors.'

'As home helps?'

'Don't be silly. As clients.'

Jane grinned. 'I like it, I like it! What services will you provide?'

'Domestic ones—so wipe the smirk off your face! And may I also remind you that single women will qualify too?' Diana finished the sandwich she had been eating when her friend arrived, and pushed away the plate. 'I'll need money to rent and equip a decent office, and rather than borrow from the bank, I shall sell up here and move into a bedsitter.' The word brought memories of Adam flooding back, and she fell silent.

'Stop thinking of that pig,' Jane ordered, sensitive to her mood. 'Haven't you got over him yet?' Not waiting for an answer, she rushed on. 'If you went out more— didn't freeze out your old friends—you'd meet someone else and forget him.'

'First, I'd like to put my life in order.'

'Exactly. Get married!'

Diana laughed. 'It's more important for me to be independent.'

'If that's how you feel, then the sooner you get cracking the better.'

Diana did.

She enrolled in a three-month intensive business studies course, put her apartment on the market and gave notice to her two employers, who promised to recommend her agency when she opened it.

All her plans slid smoothly into place. She obtained a higher price than she had expected for her home, found a room close to the college she was attending, and for the duration of her course did not lift her head from her books or her computer.

Finding suitable office premises was the big problem, for she wanted a prestigious address. But the rents in Belgravia or Kensington were astronomical, and she was on the verge of settling for a single room at the wrong end of the King's Road, when Jane's brother Hugo found her a suite of offices at a reasonable rental, in the same building as his estate agency.

'I wish you had a better place to live,' Jane commented when Diana, on signing the lease, invited her over to dinner. 'Staying in a dump like this would give me the creeps.'

'How tactful you are!'

'I've been tactful with you far too long. Now I'm going to be honest! For the first time in years you have money in the bank and you can afford something better than this. Hugo knows of a studio apartment you can get for an absolute snip.'

Diana shook her head. Since the loss of her father's fortune she had vowed not to owe money to anyone, and while it had entailed sacrifices during the past years, her peace of mind had made it worthwhile.

'Once I've made a go of my agency, I'll move. But until then, I'd rather preserve my assets. Then if things don't pan out, I won't have commitments I can't afford.'

'Fair enough. But the minute you start making decent profits, I'll start nagging!'

Jane could have done so within three months, for Bachelor's Helpline took off like a rocket. Cleverly worded advertisements for staff drew an excellent response, and Diana carefully screened each applicant, bluntly informing them she was not running a dating service, and that any member of her staff would be dismissed if they became 'friendly' with a client. But she also made it plain to her clients that she would not tolerate sexual harassment of her staff, and the few who tried were removed from her books.

Because she paid more than the going rate she secured the best help, and charged her clients accordingly. If they balked at the cost, she suggested they look elsewhere, for there was no shortage of people willing to pay over the odds for a reliable service. Indeed, keeping it reliable frequently necessitated Diana filling in herself when a 'daily' was off sick and a replacement couldn't be found.

Since this meant leaving the office unattended, she engaged a young girl to act as receptionist cum secretary.

Kathy Markham was bright and efficient, and Diana was free to concentrate on expanding her agency. She had just put down the receiver after making an appointment to meet the manager of a block of service flats off Lowndes Square—he was hoping she would take over the care of them—when the telephone rang again.

'Diana?' a lilting American voice enquired.

'Yes?' Not recognising the speaker, Diana frowned. 'Who are you?'

'Claudia, you idiot! Claudia Andrews.'

Diana was astounded. Claudia had been one of her closest friends at finishing school in Switzerland, and had returned home to New York professing undying love and the promise to keep in touch. Inevitably they had lost contact, and it was years since they had last had any contact.

'How marvellous to hear from you, Claudia. When did you get here and how did you find me?'

'I've been here a week and I was given your number by a friend of yours called Jane. I met her at a dinner party last night, and on the off-chance asked if she knew you. I tried your old number the first day I arrived, and the foreigner who answered didn't know who I was talking about!' The lilting voice slowed. 'I was sorry to hear about your mother. Jane told me, and filled me in on the rest of the story. It must have been hell for you.'

'It's over and forgotten.' Diana made light of it. 'Tell me about yourself. How long are you here for?'

'Forever, I hope. Six months ago I met a gorgeous man in Chicago, who's now extending his business to England, so I persuaded the public relations company I work for to assign me to their London branch.'

'Good thinking!'

Claudia laughed. 'I've also wangled myself a sensational apartment in Mayfair—it belongs to one of our clients who's living in Rio for a year—and I'm counting on you to move in with me.'

'You must be joking!'

'*You're* joking if you think I'll let you live in a furnished room, when I have bags of space here.'

'Jane shouldn't have told you.' Diana was angry and did not hide it.

'Don't be annoyed with her,' Claudia pleaded. 'She's a good friend and wants the best for you. And moving in with me *is* the best. We'll have such fun, Di. Do say yes.'

Diana was tempted, yet reluctant to give up her hard-won independence, and was wondering what to say when Claudia spoke again.

'At least come and stay for a few months. Living together will be like old times.'

'Won't I be in the way? If you have a boy-friend——'

'At the moment he's commuting between here and the States. He's English by the way, but has been in Chicago for years. He's just bought a place of his own in London, and once he starts spending more time here, I probably *will* ask you to leave. But until then, you'll be doing me a favour. And Adam too. He thinks I'll get up to mischief if I live alone!'

'Adam?' Diana's heart skipped a beat.

'Adam Morgan, my DIY tycoon.'

'What sort of a tycoon is a DIY?'

'He owns a Do-It-Yourself conglomerate. A thousand stores across the States.'

'Of course. DIY. Idiotic of me not to realise the obvious!' Diana drew a shaky breath of relief. For one dreadful moment she had been scared it was *her* Adam.

'Let's get back to you, honey,' Claudia went on. 'You're moving in with me, and that's final. Which reminds me, what's your name now?'

'I reverted to my own after the divorce.'

'Very sensible. At least you won't be reminded of him any more! Pity I wasn't here when you met him. I can smell a louse a mile off.'

'He wasn't a louse,' Diana defended. 'Simply obstinate and rigid.'

'Stupid too, from what Jane said.'

'She hardly knew him.'

'She knew how he behaved! I admire your loyalty, Di, but face facts. The guy behaved like a possessive fool and didn't even have the decency to get in touch with you when your father died. And then to disappear without a word... Believe me, you're well rid of him.'

Diana remained silent, aware that Claudia, only a year older than herself but born worldly-wise, would never have fallen for an impecunious, ambitious young man too proud to take help, too proud to concede he could ever be in the wrong.

'How soon can you move in?' Claudia asked.

'How soon do you want me?'

'As of now! No point standing on the diving board looking at the water. Plunge in, I say.'

So it was that later that day Diana and four cases stood outside the door of her friend's apartment in Grosvenor Square. A hesitant ring and she was almost instantly enveloped by a tall, voluptuous redhead smelling of Paloma Picasso perfume and wearing a black dress that was a perfect foil for her dramatic gold jewellery.

How radiant and confident she is, Diana thought, taking in the pert-featured face, with its slightly too large mouth, and slightly too small hazel eyes skilfully enhanced by two different tones of eyeshadow. Claudia

had always been an attractive girl, but now she was
stunning, and definitely a New Yorker.

'It's fabulous seeing you.' Diana hugged her tight, then
stepped back. 'You look like a million dollars!'

'I wish I could say the same about you.' Claudia drew
her into the parquet-floored hall and closed the door.
'You're so thin and pale. Still, it's nothing a sun lamp
and a few extra pounds won't cure.'

'You're jealous of my nice flat bottom in jeans!' Diana
made herself laugh. 'As for being pale—*Vogue* says it's
this year's look.'

Claudia caught her hand and led her past the lounge—
tastefully but anonymously furnished with modern
settees, wall-to-wall carpeting, and toning satin drapes—
to the end of the hall where there were two bedrooms
with en-suite bathrooms. Diana's was the smaller of the
two, but twice as large as her bedsitter, and any mis-
givings she had about accepting her friend's invitation
vanished at sight of the luxuriously appointed bathroom,
with its jacuzzi tub and mirrored walls and ceiling.

'Beats the bedroom we shared at Madam Victoria's,'
Claudia joked about their finishing school as she sat in
Diana's bedroom, watching her put away clothes in the
walk-in wardrobe. 'When I think of the money the old
bag charged our parents, I'm not surprised she retired
to a penthouse in Monaco!'

It was the first Diana had heard of it and she burst
out laughing. She was still smiling as Claudia went out,
having first informed her that since Adam was in the
States at the moment, she was a bachelor girl again and
they could spend the evening catching up on each other's
news.

Diana's fears that her friend might be too prying
proved groundless, for she was too full of her own happiness to show more than a passing interest in anyone

else's misfortune. It was easy to deflect her questions and get her to talk about herself and the man she was hoping to marry who, even accounting for Claudia's bias, sounded pretty sensational.

With surprising ease Diana settled into her new surroundings. Claudia was only too willing to draw her into her circle of *émigré* Americans and 'showbiz' people who, in the main, were her clients, but Diana was often too tired to go out. Bachelor's Helpline was going from strength to strength, and she was continually engaging more 'helpers', which meant most of her days were spent interviewing and selecting, while paperwork had to be done in the evenings.

'All work and no play will make you a very dull girl,' Claudia chastised one evening, after Diana had again refused to accompany her to a party. 'If you continue at this pace you'll wear yourself into the ground.'

'Until I start making real money I can't afford to slow down.'

'You can still take a few hours off to buy some new clothes and have your hair restyled. Frankly, you're a mess.'

Diana glanced at herself in the mirror over the fireplace. There was no denying Claudia's criticism. Her charcoal jersey dress, bought in an inexpensive chain store, was three years old, and though its long, fluid lines moulded her figure, it also showed she was far too thin, in spite of having gained weight these past weeks.

'If you want to end up a rich old spinster, then fine,' Claudia scolded. 'But if you'd like to marry again you have to make an effort. There's a lot of competition out there.'

Diana shrugged, knowing that Claudia, who was unsentimental in the extreme, would not understand that since Adam—*her* Adam, not the unknown one who sent Claudia flowers every day and made long telephone calls from all over the States—she had found it difficult to interest herself in other men.

'Stop looking so miserable and get changed,' Claudia broke into her thoughts. 'You're coming with me to-night, so quit arguing!'

With a resigned shrug, Diana went to her room to shower. Because of her friend's criticism she took special pains with her appearance, knowing the pleated black silk dress she had bought in a thrift shop to attend her mother's funeral drew attention to her tiny waist and disguised the fact that her curves were not as rounded as they should be. She and Claudia made a good foil for each other; one tall, voluptuous and vivacious, the other slender as a ballerina, and with the same quiet grace.

Diana pulled a face. Quiet grace? Who was she kidding? She was dull and awkward, her confidence sapped by the callous way Adam had walked out on her. Forcing the memory aside, she carefully inched on a pair of black sheer tights and narrow black court shoes. During the lean years, shoes had been her only extravagance, but her mother had always maintained that if your legs looked good, the rest of you felt good, and Diana had found this to be true.

Swinging round to the mirror, she gathered her corn-gold hair into a thick strand, and with dextrous fingers plaited it, then let it fall down the back of her head like a golden rope. Carefully she pulled a few wisps free to curl upon her high cheekbones and, for the first time in many months, wondered what Adam would say if he saw her now.

She bit her lip in vexation, wishing Claudia's boy-friend didn't have the same name. Whenever she heard it, it brought her ex-husband to mind as she had last seen him: eyes blazing with contempt, broad shoulders held stiffly, the way they always were when he was trying to control his temper.

Her hands started to shake and she had difficulty fastening the single strand of pearls around her throat. With an indrawn sob she clasped them in her hand and looked at them. They were an eighteenth birthday present from her parents, and though she had wanted to sell them after the financial crash, her mother had made her promise she never would. They shimmered up at her, pink and lustrous, and she fingered them gently. Pearls for tears, she mused, yet tears could stand for joy too, and maybe one day they would.

Feeling calmer, she fastened them round her throat. The old Diana was gone for good, she knew; the innocence drowned by bitter experience, the joyful exuberance lost beneath tragic remembrances. Though her skin was smooth and unlined, sadness had left its mark on her face.

How perceptive I've become, she mocked herself. I'm much more the sort of girl Adam could love now. Yet in spite of her faults he had loved her once—though not enough to make allowances for her youthful mistakes, and keep their marriage going; not enough to appreciate the loyalty she had felt towards her parents.

For goodness' sake stop thinking about the past, she berated her reflection. If you don't, you won't have much of a future. Upon which injunction she picked up her purse and went out.

The party was exactly as she had feared: crowds of noisy people more interested in hearing their own voices than anyone else's, an over-abundance of plastic canapés, and rock music played too loudly.

Within half an hour she was wishing she had never come, and within an hour she left, pleading a headache.

'I'll follow you the minute I can,' Claudia promised. 'But it's the boss's party...'

Alone in the Grosvenor Square apartment, Diana slipped into a housecoat and put one of her cassettes into the recorder. The sonorous notes of the Beethoven *Fifth* resounded in the room, reminding her of the concert when Adam had stood her up. Angry that he should still insinuate himself into her thoughts—it was one of those days it seemed—she hurriedly replaced the tape with a Neil Diamond.

I'm nothing if not eclectic, she thought wryly, wandering aimlessly round the room, regretting she had left the party. At least being there had stopped her from thinking. She frowned, dismayed to realise she no longer belonged anywhere; not in the boring circle of upper-class Sloane Rangers who had comprised her past, nor among Claudia's driving, ambitious crowd.

I must try to make new friends, she decided, and knew that when she had a decent home to which she could invite people, it would be easier to widen her circle. Yet her financial position was still too tight for her to take on such a burden. Of course she'd have to leave here once Claudia's boyfriend was on the scene more permanently, but she would move back to a bedsitter—for the time being at least.

This situation presented itself more quickly than she had envisioned, for the following Saturday afternoon Adam Morgan telephoned Claudia to say he was at London Airport, and would be with her as soon as he had taken his luggage to his new apartment.

Claudia was over the moon, and Diana, reluctant to play gooseberry, immediately said she was going out.

'Skip the tact!' Claudia grinned. 'I want you two to meet each other. We'll have drinks here, then Adam and I will go out to dinner and then on to his place. I can't believe I'll be seeing him in an hour! He's so gorgeous, Di, prepare yourself for a visual treat.'

Diana delighted in her friend's joy. Although they had lost touch since they had left finishing school, these past shared months had shown her that Claudia was still the same bright warm-hearted girl, given to extravagance and emotional hyperbole. Yet what she felt for the latest man in her life was obviously serious, for she eschewed all dates and, apart from business entertaining, was content to spend evenings and weekends with Diana.

'I'm really crazy about him,' Claudia continued, echoing Diana's thoughts. 'He's everything I've ever wanted. Mind like a razor, witty, passionate, tender, and loaded!'

'Five excellent reasons for changing those baggy pants and sweatshirt for something glamorous!'

Laughing, Claudia rushed to her room, and Diana went to the kitchen and checked there was champagne in the refrigerator before setting crystal goblets on a salver. Then she went to make herself tidy. Not that the razor-minded, witty, passionate, tender and loaded Mr Morgan would have eyes for anyone other than Claudia! But the least she could do was to dab powder on her shiny nose and run a comb through her dishevelled blonde waves.

She was still in her room when she heard the doorbell ring, followed by Claudia's heels clicking on the parquet floor as she ran to answer it. This was followed by a long silence that did not require second sight to interpret! She glanced at her watch; she would give them ten minutes alone before going in.

Only as she crossed the hall did she experience a momentary depression as she compared her friend's happiness with her own bleak future. She stopped and shook her head. That was defeatist thinking. She was still young and had the best part of her life ahead. She was damned if she would go on allowing the memory of her ex-husband to ruin it.

Head high and smiling, she pushed open the living-room door and walked in, stopping dead as she saw *her* Adam drawing slowly away from Claudia's clinging embrace.

CHAPTER TWELVE

DIANA knew that for the rest of her life she would never forget the sight of Adam—the man she still loved—slowly withdrawing his arms from around Claudia.

Her skin tingled and she knew the blood had drained from her face, as it had drained from his, his expression mirroring her own disbelief.

Claudia, on an emotional high, was more inclined to chatter than to perception, and was unaware of the tension that filled the room with an almost tangible force.

'Come on in, Diana, and meet the man you've heard so much about!'

Diana tried to speak but her throat had closed. Beseechingly she looked at Adam but he also seemed to be having difficulty speaking.

'Hey, what's with the two of you?' Claudia laughed. 'You both seem tongue-tied.'

'After—after hearing someone's name for so long,' Diana said huskily, 'it's—it's sort of strange to see them in the flesh.'

'You're not what *I* expected either,' Adam understated, clearing his throat. 'Claudia said she had an old schoolfriend staying with her but she never mentioned your name.'

'I'm Diana Farrow,' she said quickly.

'Good to meet you.'

'While you're getting acquainted,' Claudia interpolated, 'I'll fetch the champagne.'

Alone with Adam, Diana searched for something to say, but words eluded her and she could only stare at him dumbly.

'I had no idea *you* were Claudia's friend,' he stated flatly. 'I'm sorry about this.'

'So am I.' On trembling legs Diana moved over to an armchair and all but collapsed into it. 'When she kept singing the praises of Adam Morgan, I never dreamt it was you.'

'Or you'd have been off and running, I suppose?'

'Naturally. It would have saved us both embarrassment.'

'I'm not embarrassed at meeting you. Merely surprised.'

Uncertain what Claudia had told him about her—if she had told him anything at all—Diana changed the subject. 'Why the different surname?'

'It's a long story. If——'

He broke off as Claudia returned, tray and goblets in one hand, champagne in the other. Taking the bottle from her, he opened it and filled the fluted glasses with such calm dexterity that Diana knew he was no novice at the task.

She was acutely aware of his devastating presence, and shattered to find she was as susceptible to it as when she had first met him. Yet a new dimension had been added to him in the six years since she had last seen him. He had acquired polish and sophistication, and it wasn't only because jeans and sweatshirt were replaced by a perfectly tailored suit that enhanced his powerful, well-proportioned body. He also exuded the self-assurance that came from confidence and success. The years had dealt kindly with him, she admitted, better than they had with her, for his skin glowed with vitality and there were no lines on his face, despite her friend's assertion that he worked harder than any man she knew.

'A toast to your return, honey,' Claudia said, raising her glass to him as he sat beside her on the sofa. 'Long may you stay!'

Diana almost choked on her drink and hurriedly lowered her goblet, inadvertently catching Adam's eye as she did. His sardonic stare told her that he knew his arrival here had deeply disturbed her, and she glared back at him for an instant before smoothing her expression. Knowing him, he was probably waiting for her to make some gaffe or other, and she'd see him in hell first!

Taking another sip of champagne, she said lightly, 'I gather you own Do-It-Yourself stores.'

'Among other things.'

'He's a genius,' Claudia added, throwing him an adoring glance. 'Thank goodness Gus Morgan was astute enough to recognise it.'

Diana raised an enquiring eyebrow. 'Gus Morgan?'

'The man who gave Adam his big chance,' Claudia explained. 'Morgan's not Adam's real name. He adopted it——'

'I'm sure Diana isn't interested in my case history,' Adam intervened.

'But I am,' she gushed, ignoring his sardonic expression. 'I adore success stories.'

'Then tell her yours, darling.' The American girl's red-tipped hand caressed his shoulder.

Diana, alert to his every move, saw his body stiffen and, though ashamed of herself, was pleased when he rose and sauntered back to the drinks trolley to pick up the champagne bottle and refill their glasses.

'Not everyone is as interested in my success as you are, sweetheart,' he chided, then looked directly at Diana. 'What do *you* do? Or are you a lady of leisure?'

Aware of the snide implication behind his question, she flushed with anger. 'How clever of you to guess!'

'Don't let her kid you,' Claudia laughed. 'Diana's just started her own business.'

Brown eyes met sapphire ones, then he gave a nonchalant shrug. 'Good for you. I hope you do well.'

'I already am.'

'How long before you get bored and opt out?'

'I don't get bored easily,' she replied, aware that he was baiting her. 'If I care for something—or someone—I stay the course.'

'Good for you. Jet setters don't usually have staying power.'

'Hey!' Claudia protested. '*I'm* a jet setter, and my staying power is phenomenal!'

'You're the exception that proves the rule,' he teased, returning to the sofa.

'So is Diana. Don't judge her by her high-society manner and snooty accent! She's had lousy luck these last few years, and she's worked her guts out to get where she is today.'

Adam's eyebrows rose. 'No help from your parents?' he enquired.

The cruelty of his question was almost Diana's undoing, and she could not control the wobble in her voice as she answered. 'They are dead.'

Momentarily he was taken aback. 'I'm sorry. I didn't know.'

She turned away from him. How could he not know about her father, at least? He had died within weeks of Adam's walking out on her, and it had been reported in all the papers.

'Losing someone you love is always traumatic.' Adam spoke again, his voice gentle. 'But life goes on, however painful at times.'

He leaned back and stretched his arm along the back of the sofa. His jacket, undone, gaped wider, showing a well-cut cream silk shirt. No chain-store buy, Diana saw, glimpsing the small, discreet initials AM sewn on the right-hand side. He had certainly changed his tune since moving into the big time, she thought cynically, remembering how scathing he had once been about people who put their initials on their belongings.

She waited to feel anger, bitterness even at how the scales had turned, with Adam moving up as she had come down. But all she felt was gladness that he had achieved the success for which he had worked so hard, though it did not lessen her hurt that he had cut her out of his life so quickly and completely.

He frowned slightly and rubbed the back of his neck, as if trying to ease some tension. It drew her gaze to his glossy dark hair and the errant waves at his nape that he could not quite eradicate. She longed to touch them, and hurriedly averted her eyes. They fell on his hands, and in anguish she recollected the tenderness with which the calloused fingers had caressed her body. There were no calluses on them today, and those smooth, supple fingers caressed another body. Pain seared through her, and it took all her will-power not to run out. But that was one satisfaction she had no intention of giving him.

'What a maudlin conversation we're having,' Claudia protested, jumping to her feet. 'We're supposed to be celebrating. I've booked a table at Le Soufflé, Adam, and I'd better change or we'll be late.'

'You're welcome to join us,' he murmured to Diana when they were alone.

'Charming of you to suggest it,' she said sweetly, 'but I don't fancy being a third wheel. Anyway, I have a date,' she lied.

'Still mixing with the same crowd?' he asked disdainfully.

'Naturally.'

'I'm surprised you aren't married.'

'I could say the same of you.'

'I've had too many other things on my mind,' he said tonelessly.

'Ah, yes, your career. That takes precedence over everything.'

'You still find that strange, don't you? But then you never understood me.'

'That's the cry of the guilty husband!' she laughed. 'I didn't expect you to be so hackneyed, Adam. You disappoint me.'

'I always did.'

'That's true. Fortunately, understanding you can now be Claudia's pleasure.'

'What pleasure?' the American girl questioned, hearing the tail-end of their conversation as she rejoined them.

'Of being an international publicist.' Diana said the first thing that came into her head. 'Adam was telling me how good you are at your job.'

'And explaining that was how we met,' he elaborated smoothly.

'He bowled me over from the word go.' Claudia smiled at him mistily. 'And I've been happily horizontal ever since!'

Diana moved abruptly and Adam saw it. 'Go easy, Claudia. You're embarrassing your friend.'

'Don't be silly, darling, she knows all about the birds and bees!'

'Are you dining out too?' Adam questioned as Claudia moved off to get her coat.

'No, I'm making dinner here.' At least that was no lie. 'Is there any more champagne?' she requested, even though she was already feeling heady. But the effort of appearing indifferent to his relationship with another woman was taking its toll, and she was beginning to dread being left alone with her thoughts.

'Isn't it wiser to wait until you've eaten something?'

'I'm used to drinking.' She held out her glass and he refilled it.

'You didn't used to be,' he said.

'That was a long time ago.'

'Six and a half years.'

'Happy anniversary, darling!' she mocked. 'Clever of you to remember.'

'Don't you?'

'Afraid not. The best way of dealing with unpleasant memories is to forget them.' She gestured vaguely and lifted her glass. But her effort at indifference played her false, for her hand shook and firm fingers reached out and took the glass from her.

'You aren't as unaffected as you pretend,' he said quietly.

Aware of him watching her like a hawk, she knew the only way to stop him guessing the reason for her agitation was to admit part of the truth. 'Seeing you has reminded me how silly and immature I was. You were right on that score, Adam. I was too young to marry.'

'I wonder if we'd have succeeded if we had met today?' he mused.

'I doubt it.' Her careless tone could have won her an academy award. 'I'm still close to my old friends and I still enjoy the social scene—which you always affected to despise. Though now that you're a man of means, perhaps you enjoy it?'

'Up to a point, yes. But I could never be at ease with the dumb crowd *you* count as friends.' He ran a hand through his hair, ruffling the front so that a lock fell forward.

The gesture was nearly her undoing, and wildly she wondered what he would do if she said she didn't rate most of her friends too highly either; if she flung herself into his arms and begged him to forgive her for having been so lacking in understanding of his pride.

Angrily she checked her thoughts. Forgive *her*? What a laugh! He was the one who should be doing the begging. How easily he had cast her out of his life, uncaring that her father had suffered a stroke and her mother had been on the edge of another breakdown. But Adam—self-righteous and opinionated as always—had not been plagued by conscience where she was concerned.

'I'd like to see you alone,' he said suddenly.

'Why? We have nothing to say to each other.'

'For old times' sake. I'll call you soon.'

Before she could say no, Claudia waltzed back, and shortly afterwards they left.

Alone, Diana went to her room and flopped on to her bed, a host of conflicting emotions assailing her. Why did Adam Morgan have to be her ex-husband, and what was the best way of coping with the situation? Of one thing she was certain. She couldn't go on living here. No way could she face seeing him with Claudia and stay unaffected by their intimacy.

'What a mess!' she exclaimed aloud, realising how angry her friend would be with both of them for pretending they were strangers to each other. But caught unawares, she had acted instinctively, and when Adam had played along with her, she had decided it would be easier to tell her friend the truth when they were alone. Unless Adam did so ahead of her.

She rolled over on to her stomach and buried her head in the pillow, hoping for the oblivion of sleep. His image grew stronger and the old sensation of love overwhelmed her. Except that it wasn't an old sensation. It was the one that had been with her from the moment she had met him; the one that would remain with her for the rest of her life, making it impossible for her to forget him and put another man in his place.

He hadn't experienced the same difficulty though. She tried to close her mind to the many intimacies Claudia had confided about their relationship. She had believed they had gone into her head and out again, but now, knowing the two Adams were one and the same, she found herself remembering every one.

The pain of it brought her to her feet, and she headed for the kitchen and the comfort of a strong cup of coffee.

She was in bed but wide awake when she heard the distant thud of the front door, and within a moment her friend tiptoed into the room and whispered her name.

'I'm awake,' Diana said, and switched on the lamp beside her, amazed to see it was barely ten o'clock.

'What a let down,' Claudia grimaced, perching on the foot of the bed. 'Adam was tired, would you believe, and wanted an early night?'

'That's not surprising. He has jet lag.'

'It's only five in the afternoon, his time! If he suffered from jet lag—which he doesn't anyway—he'd be getting it tomorrow morning.'

Diplomatically, Diana kept silent.

'I had the impression you didn't like him,' Claudia went on, changing the subject with her usual rapidity. 'Just as well, though. I'd scratch out your eyes if you fell for him!'

'There's something I——' On the verge of confession, Diana stopped. Adam had obviously not come clean, and if *she* disclosed the truth before he did, he would think she had done it to create mischief; he might even think she was jealous!

'What were you going to say?' Claudia asked.

'Nothing.'

'Are you tired, or do you want to chat a while? I promised to tell you why he changed his name.'

How can I listen and pretend she's referring to a stranger? Diana thought in panic. But curiosity won, and she nodded. 'I'm not tired.'

'Well, his real name is Adam Brooke. At least that's the name that was pinned to his shawl when he was left outside a church.' Claudia settled herself more comfortably, tucking long legs beneath her. 'He never knew who his parents were, and was brought up in an orphanage. He was studying at night college, and working in a gasoline station by day, when he met Gus Morgan. Can you imagine Adam as a pump attendant?' she smiled. 'I wish I could have seen him.'

Diana nearly said *she* had, but caught herself in time.

'Anyway, as I was saying, Gus Morgan came into the garage to get a tyre fixed, and took a fancy to him. All above board, incidentally. Turned out he was an orphan too, so he felt they had something in common. He invited him to come and work for him in the States, but Adam refused; said he knew nothing about running stores and wasn't interested in learning. Then a few months later he changed his mind and accepted the offer.'

Diana had no need to ask why. He must have decided to make a clean break after walking out on her, and what better than to go to a new country and a new career? He had clearly taken the American's surname to flatter him, which was the only thing that surprised her, for it wasn't something the Adam of old would have done.

'He always says Gus was more like a father to him than an employer,' Claudia went on. 'I guess that's why he worked his guts out for him. In less than two years Adam trebled the profits and was made managing director. Seems he had a flair for business, and couldn't put a foot wrong. Then eighteen months ago Gus died and left everything to him. He said he regarded Adam as a son, and hoped that one day he'd take the name

Morgan. Adam said when the lawyer read that out, it was one of the saddest moments of his life.'

'Why?'

'Because Gus hadn't made the request when he was alive, so he could have known how proud Adam was to be asked to bear his name. He said Gus was the only person to make him feel part of a family.'

Tears flooded Diana's eyes and she blinked rapidly to stop them falling. She knew only too well how he must have felt to suddenly find he was loved as a son.

'Well, that's the story,' Claudia said, yawning she went to the door. 'Cute, isn't it?'

'Cute,' Diana echoed, surprised that her friend had no conception of the depth of emotion behind an old man's request, and Adam's acceptance of it.

How wrong she had been to think he had taken the name Morgan for expediency. She had been bitter when he had judged *her* without knowing the facts, yet she had done the same tonight.

Had her friend been quoting him directly when she had said Gus Morgan was the nearest thing to family he had ever known? Though aware he had never regarded her parents with any affection, it was painful to know he had been so dismissive of his relationship with *her*. Had she meant so little to him?

It was pointless trying to guess the answers. Adam was no longer her husband and would, if Claudia had anything to do with it, soon be someone else's.

CHAPTER THIRTEEN

ENTERING her office next morning, Diana was greeted by a flustered secretary.

'We have an emergency,' Kathy explained. 'Mrs Barnes phoned in to say she won't be available for ten days—her little boy's sick—and I'd arranged for her to be interviewed by a new client who wants help urgently. He's chairman of Lowson Industries.'

'Everyone wants help urgently,' Diana muttered.

'Don't knock it! That's why we're going from strength to strength.'

'And I'm going from exhaustion to nervous breakdown!'

Kathy's pert face grew alarmed. 'I'll see if I can contact Marla.' She named a young Filipina who was one of their treasures.

'No, don't. She's filled in for us five times this month, and she deserves a break. *I'll* stand in for Mrs Barnes.'

'You deserve a break too.'

'I agree. But I'm the boss and the buck stops here! Give me all the details.'

Kathy's dark head bent over her notebook. 'It's a penthouse overlooking Regent's Park. A daily cook-housekeeper required to take full responsibility. Has to be tip-top as our man is extremely fussy; but money is no object.'

'Mrs Barnes may not fit the bill anyway,' Diana mused. 'And we haven't anyone else to spare at the moment. I'll have to do it myself until we can find someone.'

'That's crazy!'

'It would be crazier to turn it down.' Diana couldn't help grinning at her secretary's expression. 'Until I opened this agency I was a full-time daily for five years, so doing it for a few weeks now won't kill me. And you're quite capable of running the office.'

'Even so...' Kathy shook her head. 'Shall I call a cab?'

'I'll flag one down outside. Be an angel and call Jane and say I can't make lunch. What's the client's name?' she called from the doorway.

'Gordon Cutler. Very classy accent, and charming with it. If I were you, I wouldn't tell him you're the boss. We don't want him thinking we have so few helpers that *you* have to double as a daily!'

'Good thinking. Carry on like this and I'll open a branch office and put you in charge!'

'You catch on quick,' Kathy grinned, handing her an agency card on which she had written the address.

Her destination proved to be an ultra-modern grey stone building—one of several offering million-pound-plus apartments overlooking the park. It was as architecturally anonymous as its neighbours, its only redeeming feature the generous curved balconies, banked with plants that bespoke the same professional expertise as the profusion of greenery in the pink and green marble entrance hall.

A disembodied male voice answered the buzzer and let her in, though she still had to pass the gimlet eye of the uniformed porter manning the desk.

'The second lift's for the penthouse,' he informed her. 'It goes to the top only.'

Within seconds Diana emerged on to the fourteenth floor, a spacious expanse of black and white marble floor and white marble walls, on which hung several magnificent examples of Picasso's early period. The largest was slightly obscured by the figure of an immaculately dressed man in his late thirties, who eyed her with obvious astonishment.

Diana understood why. Normally she wore a tailored skirt and blouse for work, but having agreed to lunch with Jane—and because meeting Adam had sent her ego down to zero—she had donned one of her nicer thrift outfits: a silk knit suit that almost matched her corn-gold hair. Only as she saw her reflection full-length in the bedroom mirror had she remembered that Adam had always liked her in yellow.

'My dancing daffodil,' he had teasingly called her. The memory had been so painful that she had almost changed into something else. Only pride had prevented her. Adam might have returned to her life but he damned well wasn't going to control it!

The man in front of her moved a step closer and extended his hand. 'I'm Gordon Cutler. And you are?'

'Diana Farrow.'

She gave him the agency card and he took it and smiled at her, immediately appearing younger and less intimidating. Though he wasn't 'dishy', Kathy's favourite word to describe fanciable men—he was too ascetic-looking and punctilious in manner to qualify—he was definitely handsome in Diana's book. He was tall and slim, and his smooth fair hair lay sleek over a well-shaped head. He had the narrow, precise features often found in upper-class Englishmen, though his eyes, a clear pale grey, were unusual and very attractive. Not as attractive as Adam's, but—damn him for coming back into her life!

'Are you cordon bleu trained?' Gordon Cutler enquired, his accent as languid and drawling as that of any Regency romance hero.

'Not officially,' she replied. 'But I can honestly say I'm the same standard.'

'Excellent. Also, whatever you prepare has to be from organic foods when possible.'

'That won't be a problem. Just let me know when you're dining here, and——'

'No, no!' The man's thin but nicely shaped mouth curved in a smile. 'I'm afraid I've confused you. *I* don't live here, Miss Farrow. My chief does.'

'I see.' Diana was irritated by her stupidity. If she'd been thinking clearly she'd have realised that Lowson Industries was hardly likely to be owned by a Mr Cutler. 'If you'd be kind enough to show me round?' she suggested.

The apartment was as luxurious as she had expected, and an art lover's dream, with three memorable Renoirs, an outstanding Monet, and the best of German Expressionism—Emil Nolde, Kandinsky, August Macke and Klee. The main reception areas were marble-floored but softened by thick handmade rugs that subtly echoed the colours of the paintings; the furniture was Italian modern at its best—low, squashy sofas and easy chairs in pastel shades of softest leather; steel and smoked-glass occasional tables, and steel and gold sculptural lamps.

The four bedrooms with en-suite bathrooms, which she glanced at briefly, had been decorated by the same hand, and were elegant and faintly austere, with little concession to femininity, while the kitchen was a high-tech functional dream—or nightmare—depending on one's viewpoint. Definitely not for Mrs Barnes. Indeed, the more she imbibed the atmosphere here, the more positive she was that she had to find someone very special to satisfy the owner.

'Have you been in this line of work long?' Gordon Cutler questioned as they returned to the living-room.

'A few years,' she answered non-committally, sitting down as he motioned her to a chair. On her left, wall-to-wall sliding glass doors revealed a colourful roof garden overlooking Regent's Park, complete with mini waterfall trickling into a lily-strewn pond. As she dragged her eyes away from it, they fell on a bronze sculpture of a bird. Or was it a leaf?

'It's a Brancusi,' the man said. 'Do you like it?'

'Very much, though I'm not sure what it is.'

'A bird. But does it matter? The important thing is to enjoy the pleasure it gives you, not analyse it.'

'That's good advice,' she smiled. 'Thank you.'

'Don't thank *me*. I was quoting my employer.'

'He's a man of discernment,' she murmured, looking round. 'He has a superb art collection.'

'He inherited it—lucky devil! *My* father collects china birds! Extremely valuable, but not to my taste.'

Diana laughed, the creamy curve of her neck revealed as her head tilted back. Only as she became aware of the admiring glint in the eyes watching her did she hastily compose herself, recollecting this was not a social visit.

As if aware of her discomfort, Gordon Cutler reverted to the business in hand. 'You will be expected to keep the apartment in perfect order, do the shopping and cooking and arrange for any outside help you may require to ensure things run smoothly. If any large parties are given, you may engage outside caterers. I will let you have a list of the best ones.'

'Fine.' She hesitated. 'I don't do laundry, Mr Cutler.'

'That isn't expected. But choose a hand one for all personal clothes and table linen. Which reminds me, when the chief dines alone he likes simple meals, and either my secretary or myself will give you his weekly itinerary.'

Diana swallowed her amusement, though she didn't quite manage to hide a smile.

'May I share the joke?' the languid voice enquired.

An imp of mischief decided her to be honest. In these past miserable years she had swallowed so much that, now she was her own boss, it was a pleasant change not to have to watch every word. The worst that could happen was that she lost out on this job, but with so many available, it wouldn't be a hardship.

'I was merely wondering if I'll be allowed to speak to my employer, or if I'll only be allowed to communicate with him via a fax machine or yourself.'

There was a startled silence, then the man laughed: a full-blooded sound, totally unlike his precise and elegant appearance. 'Looks as if I've given you the wrong impression of the chief. But I'm so determined to have everything the way he likes it that it's made me paranoid!'

'Is he so difficult to work for, then? I'd appreciate the truth, Mr Cutler.'

'He's dead easy to work for as long as you follow the few rules he insists on. And the most important ones—other than the few I've already given you—are that his home must always look lived-in, even when he's abroad. That means fresh flowers in the reception rooms and the main suite, fruit on his bedside table and the living-room, and a well-stocked refrigerator.'

'Isn't that wasteful?'

The warmth slightly evaporated from the face opposite her. 'Wasteful or not, that is what we require.'

Privately, Diana thought that even if she filled this place with flowers and fruit it wouldn't look lived-in. The décor was too austere, the hand of the designer too obvious. Still, to say so would definitely land her out on her ear!

'Do you wish me to start work today?' she asked instead.

'No. A few of the kitchen cabinets are being changed, and the fitters will be here most of the afternoon. But you will be paid for today.'

'That won't be necessary.'

'I doubt if your agency would agree! I've taken up your time and prevented them sending you out on another job. Please have them bill us.' He picked up a bunch of keys from the table next to him. 'These are for the apartment and the main entrance. They are all marked.'

'What time do I start?'

'Early, I'm afraid. Seven-thirty. The chief likes a cooked breakfast at eight sharp.'

'Organic bacon?' she murmured, straight-faced.

'Eggs and bacon, or smoked kippers or haddock—we have them sent from Scotland.' The answer was as dry as her question. 'Preceded by the usual—fresh fruit juice, porridge, granary toast.'

'If I have to start so early I won't stay to serve an evening meal, though I'll prepare it, of course, ready to heat in the microwave.' Her eyebrows drew together in a frown. 'To be honest, you might find it more satisfactory to engage a live-in housekeeper.'

'The chief doesn't like staff underfoot.'

'In an apartment this size, he wouldn't even know anyone was here!'

'Possibly. But I'm sure you'll do perfectly. Most business entertaining is done at a private club, and when there's a dinner party here—which is usually once a month—you may engage any extra staff you require. Most days you may leave as soon as you've finished, and the time you take is up to you. We won't check your hours, and will pay for five full days.'

'That's very generous.' The old boy must be loaded, Diana thought. 'Did you hear of our agency through an advert?'

'No, from a friend—Tony Garner. He praised it to the sky.'

Diana couldn't help feeling pleased, and Gordon Cutler noticed it.

'Your look of pride reflects a good boss. We have that in common,' he remarked. 'The only thing that puzzles me is why you aren't doing something more rewarding.'

'Running a home perfectly can be very rewarding. I have no complaints.'

He looked momentarily embarrassed. 'That wasn't what I meant.'

'You mean what's a nice girl like me doing in a job like this?' Diana asked forthrightly. 'I have no snobby hang-ups about what I do. I rid myself of those a long time ago.'

'You sound as if you've known better days,' came the perceptive reply. 'You intrigue me, Miss Farrow.'

'I'm very ordinary,' she denied. 'And please call me Diana.'

'Only if you call me Gordon. Don't shake your head; I thought you said you had no snobby hang-ups?'

'You're quick to spot a weak argument! Very well— Gordon.'

She rose and went to the door, acutely conscious of him as he accompanied her into the outer vestibule.

'I hope you'll have dinner with me one evening,' he said. 'You aren't engaged or anything, are you?'

'No, I'm free.' If only she felt it, instead of the aching longing for Adam that still haunted her nights. 'Quite free,' she reiterated firmly. 'But agency employees aren't allowed to fraternise socially with clients.'

'How can I be a client when we're both working for the same boss?'

'So we are! I never thought of that.'

'Then you'll have dinner with me?'

Why shouldn't she? She had no intention of spending the rest of her life crying for Adam. 'I'd like that,' she said aloud.

'Tonight?'

'Are you always so quick off the mark?'

'If the prize is worth winning. Sorry, that makes you sound like an object I'd like to get my hands on. Well, in one sense I would, but—— Hell! I'm making it worse, aren't I?'

'Much worse—but I forgive you! And I *am* free tonight.'

'Smashing. Let me know where you live and I'll call for you.'

As she gave him the élite Grosvenor Square address, she saw his gold pen pause. 'I'm temporarily staying with a girlfriend,' she explained. 'I sold my apartment and haven't yet found another one.'

He nodded. 'I'll pick you up at eight. Any preference as to food?'

'None. But could you make it seven-thirty? I prefer to eat early.' She flashed him a warm smile, hoping her request didn't sound odd, but she was anxious to avoid bumping into Adam, who was calling for Claudia at eight.

'No problem,' Gordon said. 'It means I'll be seeing you that much sooner!'

Long before the agreed time, Diana was dressed and waiting for him downstairs in the lobby. The instant she saw him emerge from his car, a sleek Jaguar, she opened the heavy glass door and hurried down the steps to meet him.

'I wasn't sure if you'd find a parking place,' she said by way of excuse.

'Very thoughtful of you.' He helped her into the car. 'I hope this augurs well for our future!'

She flashed him a smile. 'It just shows that I'm a car driver too!'

'Let's hope we have many other things in common!'

His jokey remark proved truer than either of them had anticipated, for during dinner they discovered they had several mutual friends.

'It's astonishing that we haven't met before,' he commented. 'Where have you been hiding?'

'Not hiding,' she evaded. 'Working. It's left me little time for socialising.'

'I hope that won't apply to us?'

She murmured non-committally and he did not press the point, which made her like him all the more. Jane would definitely approve of him if and when she met him. She was still badgering her to see more of their old crowd, and though Gordon didn't qualify in this respect, he did in every other, being Eton-educated, with an Oxbridge degree. She deliberated whether to give him a censored version of her past but decided against it. Time enough to do so if their friendship continued.

At eleven-thirty he drove her home. 'I'm tied up the rest of the week,' he said, 'but I hope you're free at the weekend?'

'I can see you Saturday evening.'

'Why not make a day of it? I've been invited to Wiltshire for lunch, and my hosts won't object if I bring a friend.'

Diana hesitated. She had planned to spend the day hunting for somewhere else to live, but the thought of getting away from London was more appealing. Fortunately many estate agents were open on Sunday and she could as easily do it then.

'I'd like a day away from the smoke,' she agreed.

'Good. Be ready by ten.' He leaned forward and kissed her lightly on the cheek. 'Till Saturday,' he said huskily.

Diana was still in her bathroom removing her make-up when Claudia arrived home, starry-eyed and walking on air.

'I'm going away with Adam for the weekend,' she announced.

Diana's pleasurable mood disappeared beneath a flood of jealousy, but she managed to keep control of her voice. 'A few relaxing days will do you good.'

'Relaxing? Not if I know lover-boy! He's dynamite in bed.'

Remembering the intensity of their own lovemaking, Diana knew Claudia wasn't exaggerating. Even during the worst days of their marriage, Adam's ardour had never diminished, and with hindsight she had often wondered if the strength of his passion had delineated a need to make up for their lack of communication elsewhere.

'How was your date?' Claudia enquired. 'I found your note saying you were going out. I must have missed you by five minutes.'

'It was fine. Very successful, in fact. I'm seeing——'

Claudia's yawn cut her short, and she reached for her toothbrush, amused rather than irritated by her friend's egoism. It was just as well to end the conversation. Further talk of boyfriends might encourage more discourse on Adam's sexual prowess, and send her screaming from the room.

Predictably, her sleep was fitful, and she was tired and listless as she showered and dressed at six-thirty next morning. No sight to tempt Gordon today, she thought wryly as she went out to her car. Her taupe shift was an excellent colour for vibrant blondes sporting masses of gold chains, but did nothing for an overworked blonde with lifeless hair and colourless skin. Luckily the pink and white candy-striped apron—the standard uniform for her agency home helps—would make her look less like a ghost.

Gordon had said there were two parking spaces available to the penthouse in the garage below the block, and she could use one of them until further notice. As she drew into the only empty bay, she glanced admiringly at the sedate grey Rolls Bentley in the next slot. This year's model, she noted as she stepped out of her old Renault. Its quiet elegance was on a par with the penthouse, and probably typified Mr Lowson's character. Was there a wife somewhere in the background? Very far in the background if his home was anything to go by. Or perhaps he didn't like women!

Letting herself into the apartment, she went directly to the kitchen. With the morning sun flooding the room, it was less austere, though nothing could soften the appearance of the steel-grey kitchen cabinets and the paler granite tops. Talk about an operating theatre! It was also as perfectly equipped, with Rosenthal china and cutlery and Waterford glassware. Only the refrigerator was bare. American, with triple doors and automatic ice maker, it contained a carton of milk and a bowl of apples. Later today she would do a large shop, but for breakfast she could manage with the food she had bought on her way home yesterday afternoon.

Methodically she prepared breakfast, grinding the coffee beans and placing them in the percolator, setting the porridge to simmer, and placing three slices of granary bread in the toaster, before going into the adjoining dining-room to set the table.

Here, a mirrored wall was used with dramatic effect, reflecting a huge David Hockney painting of the artist and friends beside a swimming pool. Nineteenth-century neo-classical chairs provided seating around a long table of the same design, and the soft Wedgwood green of the walls was repeated in the hand-washed Chinese carpet.

Returning to the kitchen to squeeze fresh orange and mango juice into a crystal glass jug, she felt a growing curiosity to meet the man who lived here. Lowson Industries must be highly successful to support this lifestyle. She half smiled. According to Gordon, Mr Lowson had inherited most of the paintings she had seen here, which meant he had started his career with millions behind him. A distinct advantage!

A glance at her watch warned her it was two minutes to eight, and she placed the jug of juice on the table and set the silver tureen bowl of porridge on the hot plate on the sideboard. It seemed a pity to prepare the bacon and eggs ahead of time too, since there was only one person to cook for, and she returned to the kitchen and switched the grill to low before opening the refrigerator to take out two eggs. The apples caught her eye and she bent to take one. As she did, she saw a pair of tanned bare feet in suede moccasins behind the door. Heavens! Did her employer make a habit of creeping up on people?

Hurriedly stepping back, she closed the door and straightened, her eyes taking in the broad-shouldered figure in the short black bathrobe. Apple and eggs fell from her nerveless fingers to the floor, and speechlessly she stared into the strong-boned face.

'What the hell are *you* doing here?' Adam demanded.

CHAPTER FOURTEEN

DIANA and Adam stared at each other, and it was hard to say who was the more shocked.

Diana wished the floor would open and swallow her. Of all the men she could have gone to work for, why oh, why did it have to be him?

Glittering brown eyes raked her from head to toe, taking in her pale face and severely pinned back hair—no risk of golden ones falling into the food—her serviceable dress almost hidden by the pink candy-striped apron, and her flat shoes, which made him tower over her.

'Don't tell me *you're* the new housekeeper?' he questioned incredulously.

'Temporarily only.'

'You can say that again! Gordon said he hired a cordon bleu. I wasn't aware they did a course in burnt offerings!'

Angered by the heavy sarcasm, she did her best not to let it show. 'That was a long time ago—I've learned a lot since then.'

'I hope so—you had a lot *to* learn.'

She did not rise to his baiting. Fresh from the shower, his hair was still slightly damp and curled over the collar of his black robe instead of lying smoothly against the nape of his neck. It made him appear younger and less of the tycoon, and she took heart from it. This was the man she had married, slept with, made love with. He was no ogre set to destroy her. Leastways only her peace of mind, she admitted raggedly, stifling the urge to run her hands through the thick, silky strands of his hair, and to press herself against his lean, muscled body.

Instead, she found a cloth under the sink and bent to wipe up the mess of eggs on the floor.

'I'll do it,' he said brusquely, reaching to take the cloth from her hand.

'No, thanks, it's *my* job.'

Competently she cleaned the floor, dropped the cloth into the smaller of the two sinks, and washed her hands. All the while she was conscious of him watching her every move, and marvelled that she managed to act as though it was an everyday occurrence to prepare breakfast for her ex-husband, who was also the lover of the girl she was living with!

'I thought Claudia said you'd started a business?' Adam spoke again. 'I hardly think working as a ''daily'' qualifies.'

'I run a domestic agency called ''Bachelor's Helpline'',' Diana answered carefully. 'The only reason I'm here is that we're so successful, we're short-staffed. With luck, you won't have to put up with me for long. As soon as I find a suitable replacement, I'll leave.'

'It doesn't bother me having you around. But it might be embarrassing for *you*.'

'Not especially,' she lied. 'I have no hang-ups about what I do. It's honest and well paid. You aren't the only one who's changed, Adam. I have too.'

He gave a thin smile. 'I haven't changed much—just made a stack of money.'

'With a little help from a friend,' she couldn't help adding.

'I see Claudia's filled in the gaps.' He was unruffled.

'Some of them.' She moved to the refrigerator. 'One egg or two?'

'Two please, lightly turned, with three slices of toast placed in a toast rack.'

At least *that* was the same. He'd always loathed soggy toast. 'Your juice and porridge are in the dining-room. I'll bring in the bacon and eggs in five minutes.'

'I'm quite happy to eat in the kitchen.' He perched on one of the bar stools, and as he did his bathrobe parted, revealing strongly muscled legs.

Wondering if he was naked underneath, and disturbed by the possibility, she darted into the dining-room and brought back the porridge and fruit juice. While he ate, she prepared the bacon and eggs, placed them on a warmed plate, and set it in front of him.

'Looks good,' he remarked. 'Why don't you join me?'

Her first instinct was to refuse, but she wanted to discuss Claudia with him, and this was an ideal opportunity. Perching on a stool opposite him, she poured herself a cup of coffee.

He slid the toast rack towards her but she shook her head. 'I'm not hungry.' How could she eat when sitting close to him like this made her yearn for his touch, the taste of his mouth, the weight of his body on hers?

'Like old times,' he commented.

'The only resemblance is that we're sitting at the same table,' she responded drily.

'Does it bother you?'

'Let's just say if I'd known this was your apartment, I wouldn't be here. My secretary was only given the name of your company, which meant nothing to me, and Gordon simply referred to you as his chief.'

'Gordon, is it now?'

Delighted she had provoked him into this comment, she said casually, 'Mr Cutler would have been rather formal across a dinner table. I meant to ask him who you were last night, but I forgot. He went to school with several of my old boyfriends and we had fun reminiscing.'

'He's a nice chap—and like me, managed to rise above his background! You could do a lot worse,' Adam added, draining his cup and rising. 'As you probably guessed, he's no ordinary personal assistant. His father's Lord Cutler, and Gordon's heir to the title and the stately pile. Just what your parents always wanted for you!'

'If I'd wanted it for myself, I wouldn't have married *you*,' she pointed out. 'I believed in marrying for love, and that still hasn't changed.'

'But your circumstances have. It's easy to marry for love when you have rich parents.' He caught hold of her hand before she could stop him and ran a finger over the slightly roughened skin, and the short nails bare of varnish. 'You may have your own business but you can't be making a fortune.' Stepping back slightly, he studied her. 'The apron's pretty and suits you, but the dress looks as if it's seen better days.'

Diana went scarlet. She didn't need Adam to remind her she wasn't the spoiled, pampered beauty he had married. In fact she didn't need him to remind her of anything. He had forfeited that right when he divorced her.

'It would hamper my cleaning if I wore my Ralph Lauren!' she snapped.

His smile did not reach his eyes, which remained cold and searching. 'When was the last time you bought a new outfit? The truth, Di.'

The use of his pet name for her startled her, and did the same to him, if his increased colour was anything to go by.

'My agency has only been going a few months, and I'm ploughing all my profits into advertising,' she informed him. 'A year from now, I hope I won't have to penny-pinch nor help out like this.'

'For old times' sake, I'd be happy to make you an interest-free loan,' he offered laconically.

Again he was baiting her and she resisted the urge to hit out at him. 'A quarter of a million would come in handy,' she replied with equal laconicism.

'That wouldn't present a problem, if you're really serious.'

'I'm not. But thanks for the offer.' She started clearing the table, glad she could legitimately turn her back on him. 'Times have certainly changed for you, Adam, though I'm sure your success has as much to do with your ability as the luck of meeting Gus Morgan.'

'Thank you. I'm not so modest that I'll deny it! Once Gus gave me free rein, I trebled the profits in a year.' It was a statement; matter-of-fact, confident, with no hint of boastfulness.

'Don't you regret not finishing your engineering course?'

'Not any more.'

'How many stores do you have?'

'More than a thousand, and we've just taken over a big chain here. Didn't Claudia tell you that too?' he asked in a slightly mocking tone.

'She was too busy informing me how fabulous you were,' Diana said deliberately.

'She's biased.'

'I know. Women in love often make fools of themselves.'

He chuckled, not one whit put out. 'You're sharp today—and it's only eight-thirty!'

'Lay the blame on a sleepless night.'

His eyes narrowed. 'Does seeing me again disturb you?'

'Not in the least. But we have to be honest with Claudia. She's never said anything to me about your having been married, and I——'

'She knows I'm divorced—I haven't made a secret of it—but I've never discussed my ex-wife with her. Our marriage is a part of my life I prefer not to dwell on,' he said flatly.

'Haven't you told *anyone* about us?'

'Only Gus Morgan.'

Adam came to stand next to her by the dishwasher, exuding a strength that made her meltingly aware of his masculinity. He smelled faintly of aftershave, not the musky one she remembered, but something pleasantly astringent, beneath which was the more intimate scent of the man himself: warm and earthy, and intensely alluring.

The longing to be held in his arms threatened to overcome her reason, and terrified that desire might turn to deed, she side-stepped him and went back to dust the table.

'I hope Claudia won't be devastated when she learns of our relationship.' Diana glanced at him over her shoulder. 'To quote her directly, she thinks my husband was a possessive fool and a louse, and I was well rid of him!'

Adam's wide mouth thinned, and Diana knew she had succeeded in annoying him.

'If she heard *my* side, she'd think differently.'

'Well, now you'll have a chance to tell her!'

'I doubt if that will be necessary,' he said. 'When she discovers I'm the ex in question, she'll realise there are two sides to every break-up.'

Diana returned to the sink and began to wash the frying-pan. She had no intention of telling him she had jumped to his defence when Claudia had been critical—he wouldn't believe it anyway.

'They say there are always three sides to a break-up,' she said lightly. 'His, hers, and the truth!'

He shrugged. 'I'll talk to her tonight. The sooner she knows the better.' He paused on the threshold. 'By the way, don't prepare an evening meal. We'll be dining out.'

She nodded, and blindly continued washing the pan; but not so blind that her mind's eye didn't conjure up a picture of Claudia coming back here with him, sharing his bed, lying in his arms. It was agony to think of it, yet she could think of nothing else.

She was still cleaning the pan—it was going to be the shiniest in Christendom!—when he returned, immaculate in a superbly fitting dark grey suit, white silk shirt, maroon tie, black calf Gucci loafers and gold Rolex Oyster watch.

'Here's some money.' He placed several fifty-pound notes on the kitchen table. 'From next week, contact Mrs Evans, my secretary, when you need more.'

'Do you wish to see the accounts monthly or weekly?'

'I don't wish to see them at all. That's Mrs Evans's department. One other thing. I won't be requiring any meals this weekend. I'm out of town.'

It was on the tip of her tongue to say she knew, when she decided it would not be well received. 'Thank you,' she murmured instead, and breathed a sigh of relief when he left.

She was perilously close to tears but pride prevented them falling. She had shed enough over him. Keeping her mind a blank, she dusted and vacuumed the reception rooms, and ran a dry mop over the marble floors. Then drawing a deep breath she went down the corridor to Adam's bedroom.

When she had seen it yesterday it had been the room of a stranger; today it was where her husband—no, her ex-husband—slept, dreamed, made love to Claudia. She bit her lip. The ramifications of working here, even temporarily, suddenly hit her, and she knew that if she couldn't find someone suitable within a week, she'd put her treasured Filipina here and take over the girl's other job.

This decision made, she felt considerably better, though her mood plummeted the instant she set foot in Adam's room. Drawn to the king-sized bed as if by a magnet, she sank down on it. Her heart pounded like a drum, and her fingers shook as they trailed over the indent mark of his head on the grey silk pillow. With a choking cry, she picked it up and held it close, rocking backwards and forwards as though she were cradling a baby.

It was a considerable while before she was in control of herself, but her tears had been cathartic, and she was able to make the bed and tidy the room and bathroom with as little emotion as though the man who used it was a stranger to her. And in many ways he was. The Adam she had married no longer existed, in his place a sophisticated man used to giving orders, assured of his success.

Yet he was uncertain how to treat her, and they had fenced like two strangers unsure of their boundaries. Not to be wondered at really, for they had both changed, matured and, in Adam's case, found another love.

'But are you happy, Adam?' she asked aloud. 'Has success brought you joy as well as wealth?'

She would have given a great deal to know his answer.

CHAPTER FIFTEEN

DIANA was fast asleep when the crash of her bedroom door awoke her. Hurriedly switching on the lamp, she saw Claudia standing at the foot of the bed, arms flung out, eyes snapping.

'What the hell game were you playing at, not telling me Adam was the man you'd married?'

So he had kept his promise. Diana drew a shaky breath, wishing she had had the foresight to ask him exactly how much he was going to disclose about their marriage. She had given her friends—other than Jane— a guarded account of why they had parted, and did not relish Claudia knowing all the intimate details.

'It didn't dawn on me that—that your Adam was my— that it was the same man,' she said unsteadily.

'But once you saw him, how could you keep quiet? You made me feel a crass idiot.'

'I'm sorry. I know it was wrong, but I—I was so shocked I couldn't think straight. I didn't want to upset you and——'

'You think it's upset me less finding out now? Jeez! When I think of the things I said about your ex...'

'I did say you were judging him too harshly,' Diana reminded her.

'That isn't what Adam says!' Claudia flung herself into a chair. 'He takes all the blame.'

Diana was astounded. Nothing he had said to her this morning had given her that impression; indeed, she had felt he was as bitter towards her today as he had been years ago.

'He says he was too hard on you, and made no allowance for your being a spoilt and innocent nineteen-year-old,' Claudia went on. 'But he was flattered that you fancied him and he'd wanted you like crazy. Once he realised he'd made a mistake, he cut and ran. He felt it was the best way. That the worse you thought of him, the quicker you'd get over him.'

Clever, clever Adam, Diana thought bitterly as she heard his version of what had occurred. In one fell swoop he had made her appear childish and foolish, and their marriage based on nothing more than sex. Was that the only way he could live with his conscience?

'I'm for bed,' Claudia said into the silence. 'I'll be glad to put this night behind me.'

So will I, Diana silently endorsed, knowing that for her it would be another sleepless one.

Saturday dawned sunny and warm, ideal for a day in the country. She toyed with the notion of calling Gordon and pleading pressure of work—not a lie, for she had a mass of things to do in the office. Yet it wasn't work that made her reluctant to accept his invitation, but Adam, whose presence in London was casting a long shadow over her life.

'Too persistent a shadow for me to let it continue,' she admonished her reflection as she dried herself after a shower. 'Adam isn't the only one who can rebuild his future. So can I.' An image of Gordon flashed in front of her, charming, controlled, yet with more than a hint of underlying warmth.

'Just what your parents always wanted for you!' Adam had scoffed, and maybe, if given the chance, she would finally do as they would have wanted.

Belting her housecoat around her, she went down the hall to the kitchen. She heard the sound of a shower coming from her friend's room and she walked quickly past, knowing she was merely putting off what she had to say.

She returned a few minutes later, bearing a cup of coffee—strong and black the way Claudia liked it—and took it in to her.

'How did you guess?' her friend exclaimed, grasping it and sipping gratefully.

Draped in a towel, her ivory skin glistening with droplets, her short wet hair vibrantly red, she was vital and glowing, and so much like the dynamic woman Adam should have married in the first place that Diana easily understood why they were lovers.

'About last night,' Claudia apologised. 'Sorry I came on so strong. But I was knocked sideways when Adam said you were his wife.'

'*Were* being the operative word,' Diana stated.

'It still beats me why you didn't come out with it straight away.'

'I would have, if I'd known that you knew he'd been divorced. But you never mentioned it, and I felt he should be the one to tell you. Which he's now done.'

'Yes.' Claudia regarded her speculatively. 'All he'd ever said of his marriage was that it was a non-event. With fifty per cent of American marriages breaking up, it's unusual to meet a man in his thirties who hasn't been divorced.' Claudia dropped her towel and stepped into peach silk panties. 'If you didn't happen to be friend of mine, it would be a non-event for me too. As it is, I feel a real Charley for talking about him to you as if he were a stranger.'

'After six years he is,' Diana retorted. 'I knew nothing of his life after he left me, and you filled in some of the gaps.'

'If you care to know more, you only have to ask!'

Diana forced a laugh. 'I know as much as I want, thank you. As Adam said, it's over and done with.'

'I'm glad. But even so...' Claudia took a weekend case from the bottom of her wardrobe and placed it on the bed. 'I hate springing this on you, but it might be better if you moved. I mean if—if Adam stayed over any time it could be awkward. You do understand, don't you?'

'Perfectly. I was planning to leave anyway.'

'I'll be happy to help you with the rent for a flat,' Claudia offered, attempting to assuage the guilt she plainly felt. 'You can pay me back when your business starts doing better.'

Diana bit back a laugh. Suddenly everyone wanted to lend her money! 'Thanks, but I can manage.'

Claudia picked up a black lace nightgown and held it against her, moulding the soft material to her voluptuous body. 'If this doesn't drive Adam wild, I don't know what will,' she purred. 'Did he go for sexy lingerie when he was married to you?'

It wasn't a question in the best of taste, and Diana was sure her friend had asked it to show the intimacy of her own relationship with Adam. More than ever she was glad she was leaving here. The sooner the better, in fact.

'I guess his taste was less sophisticated years ago,' she murmured, resisting the urge to add that there had been no need to resort to wiles to turn him on. A look or a touch had been enough.

'When are you seeing this guy Gordon again?' Claudia questioned as she continued packing.

'Today. We're visiting friends of his in the country.'

'If you want to borrow any of my clothes, feel free.'

'You're so much taller, they'd swamp me! But thanks for the offer.'

'A cardigan or scarf then. I've a Hermès that's exactly your colouring.'

Diana shook her head. 'I bought a new outfit yesterday afternoon—*and* a scarf.'

'Wow! What brought on *that* extravagance? Or should I say who?'

'Adam,' Diana answered unthinkingly.

'Adam?' The wine-red head tilted sharply. 'You mean you saw him? When you said you'd spoken to him, I thought it was on the telephone.'

Diana could have kicked herself. Sooner or later she would have had to confess she was working at his apartment, but this morning, with her friend still sensitive over what she had learned, was definitely not the best time. Making as light of it as possible, she explained the position.

Amazingly, Claudia was in no way put out. 'Life is certainly a see-saw, isn't it? I bet you never thought, when you split with Adam, that you'd become his domestic help!'

'It's what wives frequently do!'

'But not ex ones.' Claudia clapped her hand to her mouth. 'What a tactless donkey I am.' Coming close, she caught Diana's hand. 'I'm sorry. Please forgive me.'

'Forget it. You made a normal comment, and it's silly for us to get uptight about it.'

'I agree.' Claudia hugged her. 'You're one of my best friends and I'd hate anything to come between us.'

'So would I.'

'Then we won't let it.' Claudia resumed packing. 'Wouldn't it be terrific if you fell for this new man in your life? It would give everybody a happy ending!'

'I've only been out with him once.'

'Once can be enough. Adam first saw me lunching with another man at Four Seasons and fell for me then and there.'

'He was always a fast worker.'

'You can say that again.'

Except that he hasn't been a fast worker with *me*, Diana remembered as she returned to her room. She had been the one to make the running, the begging almost. Embarrassment seared her as she relived the many occasions she had forced him to see her, the ploys she had adopted, the way she had trapped him into going to bed with her.

How had he described his marriage? As a non-event? With painful honesty she had to admit that for *him* it had been, for he had married her because of the baby, and when she had lost it he had stopped trying to make the marriage work. It was simple as that. As simple and as painful.

She remained in her room until Claudia left with Adam. Knowing they were spending two whole days together—and more particularly two nights—was like a knife in her guts, and she knew that if she couldn't find suitable accommodation fast, she'd move to a hotel despite the expense. It was imperative for her peace of mind that she move away from anyone in Adam's orbit, even though it would mean the end of her friendship with Claudia, as well as Gordon.

Had Adam told him the truth too? It seemed likely in the circumstances.

As she dressed, she was pleased she had splashed out on something new. It made a change from second-hand clothes, no matter how expensive they had originally been. The oatmeal cable-knit two-piece with toning pure silk blouse had cost more than she had planned to spend, but she had a weakness for Armani and, spurred on by Adam's critical comment on her appearance, she had succumbed.

Because of the subtle colour she was less sparing with her make-up, and though she knew the glow of her skin was artificial, no one else would have guessed. Her hair looked more golden and vital too, due no doubt to the expensive shampoo to which she had treated herself. She still wore it shoulder-length, but it was less curly than when she had first met Adam, its softer waves suiting a temperament that had grown gentler with the passing years. Had the fire in her gone for ever, she mused, or could another man arouse it?

She was pondering on this when Gordon called for her. Neither his manner nor conversation gave any clue whether he knew she was 'the chief's' ex-wife, and as they headed out of London he entertained her with City gossip—since starting her agency she had taken a keen interest in the financial news—and showed an intelligent awareness of the arts.

Gradually she relaxed, amusing him in return with anecdotes culled from her daily helps.

'I should imagine you could tell me some pretty hair-raising stories if you weren't so discreet,' he commented as they drove along the motorway.

'Discretion is part of my job,' she acknowledged.

'Mine too.'

She tensed, waiting for him to say more, but he didn't. Surreptitiously she glanced at him. Dressed for the country in Lovat tweed hacking jacket and cord trousers, he appeared younger than in city clothes. His change of dress was also reflected in a change of manner. No longer was he a sophisticated yuppie but a light-hearted, irreverent public schoolboy. It was this boyishness that appealed most; this and the fact that he made no sexy innuendoes nor attempted to touch her.

'Did Mr Morgan tell you I was his ex-wife?' she blurted out. The subject had to be broached and the sooner the better.

'Yes.' Narrow hands tightened on the wheel, though his voice was relaxed. 'Quite a coincidence you working for him, isn't it?'

'That must be the biggest understatement in the world!' she said forthrightly. 'Loosen up, Gordon. I'm not taping this talk!'

'I didn't imagine you were. But I'm in a somewhat tricky position.'

'I'm surprised you didn't cancel today!'

The speedometer noticeably slackened. 'That's not a very nice comment.'

'I'm bored with pretence and subterfuge.'

'Then I'll discard both and say I'd rather resign my position than stop seeing you. Not that Adam has even hinted it. Incidentally, I only call him Chief when I'm talking to employees.'

'That's me,' she said bluntly. 'If you had told me his name when I came for the interview, I'd have been prepared.'

'Would you still have taken the job?'

'Certainly. The pay is excellent and the agency, which is mine, incidentally, does very well out of it.' She hesitated, then plunged on. 'Did you know he'd been married?'

'Yes. But all he ever said was that it didn't work out, and you parted.'

'In a nutshell, yes. There's more to it than that, of course.'

'I'm not interested in the reasons,' Gordon said firmly. 'It's the person you are today that concerns me. I like you very much, Diana. I did the moment I saw you, and if you'd be happier if I were working somewhere else, just say so.'

'I don't have the right. Nor do I want it. This is only the second time I've been out with you, and——'

'We're friends,' he cut in. 'Nothing more than that until you change your mind.' Aware of her sudden tension, he lightly tapped her arm. 'Which brings me to confession time. The friends we're seeing—it isn't simply a social visit. Their house is up for sale—it's the local manor—and Adam is interested in it. I've arranged for them to meet and discuss it over lunch.'

Diana was speechless with dismay. It was a good thing too, otherwise she would have ordered Gordon to take her home immediately, which would have put paid to the cool I-couldn't-care-less-about-Adam attitude she was pretending.

'When I asked you to come here with me,' Gordon went on, 'I had no idea you and Adam were connected.'

'But you knew I was his housekeeper. Hardly the sort of person he'd want to lunch with socially.'

'Adam doesn't give a damn what work anyone does, as long as it's honest. He's the least snobbish man I know.' Gordon slowed speed again. 'I almost rang you when I learned exactly who you were, but from the way he spoke, I had the impression neither of you were worried about meeting each other.'

'Claudia mightn't be so sanguine,' Diana remarked, marvelling she should sound so calm. 'You know her, I take it?'

'Yes. Until Adam told me, I didn't realise it was her apartment you were sharing.'

'Until I find a place of my own. I'm looking tomorrow.'

'May I help? I'm free.'

'It's a tedious task.'

'As you wish.'

Gratefully she smiled at him. How easy he was to be with, unlike Adam who had always made her feel nervous and inadequate. Well, not quite always; in bed they had been equal, giving passion for passion, no holds barred. Her hands clenched in her lap and she tried not to think of him with Claudia, not to imagine the intimate holding and touching.

'The village is ahead of us,' Gordon said, breaking into her reverie. 'I think it's one of the prettiest in England.'

With relief, Diana gave her attention to its thatched cottages and genuine Elizabethan pub opposite a reeded duck pond. A small stone church cast a delicate steeple to the sky, and weeping willows shaded the periphery of a velvet-smooth green where children played. It more than lived up to Gordon's description, though Kingsleigh, the manor house Adam was interested in buying, took her by surprise. Expecting Palladian grandeur, she saw Georgian simplicity. Three storeys high, the mellow beige brick house was set in pasture land, with woods to one side of it, and gently rising hills behind.

Adam's Bentley was parked on the gravel driveway, and Diana's heart pounded uncomfortably as she followed Gordon through the open front door into a rectangular entrance hall, with polished oak floor and magnificent carved staircase.

The drawing-room was visible on their left, and could have come directly from the pages of *Country Life*, so perfect an example was it of relaxed, upper-class living. Walking over the faded but still lovely Aubusson, dotted with squashy sofas and small marquetry tables weighted with bowls of colourful garden flowers, they reached the wide stone terrace where their hosts, Lucy and Simon Goodall, both tall, fair and in their thirties, were chatting to Adam and Claudia, who were sitting together on a hammock.

One glance at her friend's face told Diana she was far from pleased at the turn of events. The wide mouth was tight with displeasure, and for an instant the hazel eyes went hard, though she recovered her equilibrium and managed a bright smile while introductions were effected. Adam's greeting was casual as he half rose and nodded, and Diana hoped her smile didn't look fixed as she nodded back.

'You're a drink behind us,' her hostess said. 'What will you have, wine or something stronger?'

'Whisky and ice for me, and white wine for Diana. She doesn't like the hard stuff,' Gordon answered for both of them as, hand light at her elbow, he guided her to a small rattan settee, and seated himself beside her.

Diana was certain his proprietorial air was premeditated, and she was grateful to him, for nothing was more guaranteed to bolster a woman's ego than to know a good-looking, eligible man fancied her.

Sipping an excellent Chablis, she let the conversation eddy around her. Inevitably her eyes wandered to Adam, talking animatedly to their host. He'd had a haircut since yesterday, and though little could be done to control the wayward dark strand that fell over his forehead, the back was cropped well short of the collar of his bottle-green sports shirt, the sleeves rolled back to disclose tanned arms lightly sprinkled with black hair. Soft beige wool trousers outlined his muscled thighs, and though he was lounging back casually, he exuded an all-male strength that diminished the other two men.

'I'll give you all the grand tour after lunch,' Lucy said at large as her husband poured another round of drinks. 'Then if Kingsleigh lives up to expectations, the men can go and have their talk, and we'll do what fancy dictates! This is Adam's first visit,' she explained to Diana. 'He fell in love with the house from photographs we sent to America.'

'How interesting.' Diana swung round to him, intent on showing he meant nothing more to her than another guest at a lunch party. 'Does that mean you're thinking of moving from London?'

'I won't be giving up the penthouse, if that's what's worrying you,' he drawled. 'Diana owns one of the best domestic agencies in London,' he explained to Lucy and Simon, 'and she has kindly made herself responsible for the smooth running of my home.'

'Lucky you.' Lucy leaned towards Diana. 'You'd be inundated if you opened a branch down here.'

'I doubt it. We only take care of single people.'

'Which she does well enough to make single people think twice before giving up that state!' Adam interpolated with a grin.

'If that were true,' Claudia said, 'I know a few young women who'd happily put her out of business!'

In the general laughter that followed, Diana rose and, glass in hand, wandered to the end of the terrace where a golden-haired retriever was sunning himself. Seeing Adam in purely social surroundings was a bad idea. His urbane manner and effortless small talk showed how far removed he was from the gruff, chip-on-the-shoulder man she had married, and reminded her of what she had lost when he left her. Yet how could one lose what one had never had? And Adam had always been a reluctant husband, though it had taken hindsight for her to see it.

'I didn't realise you were a dog lover,' Adam said, and she looked up from stroking the dog to see him beside her.

'I've wanted one since I was a child, but any type of fur gave my mother asthma.'

'You can have one when you move. Claudia says you're leaving Grosvenor Square.'

'I doubt if I'll find a place where dogs are welcome.'

'Look harder.'

'It's more a case of digging deeper.'

'Deeper?'

Angrily she straightened. 'In my pocket, Adam. Or have you forgotten what's it like to count the pennies?'

Bewildered, he shook his head. 'I didn't realise you were so strapped for cash.'

'I told you I put most of what I had into setting up and advertising Helpline.'

'Twenty thousand would do that, and surely you——'

'I had twenty-five left from the sale of our apartment.'

'Our?' His eyes became dark slits. 'You were shacked up with someone?'

For the first time it dawned on her that he didn't have a clue what had happened to her these past six years. Her life had been so traumatic, and in the beginning the newspapers so intrusive, that she had automatically assumed he had read *something* of what had transpired, even in America.

'I was "shacked up", as you put it, with my mother.'

'Ah, yes, I always did underestimate your sense of filial duty.'

Anger scorched through her and she rounded on him. 'Still bitter because you couldn't call me to heel? You're the one who should have a dog, Adam—that way you'd get blind obedience!'

Not trusting herself to say more, she bent to the retriever and resumed stroking him. Her hand was trembling and, as if aware of it, the dog half lifted his head and licked her arm. Tears blurred her eyes and she lowered her head further. If only Adam would go away. But he remained where he was.

'When did your father die?' he asked quietly.

'On the cruise.'

'That soon?'

'Yes. We buried him in Australia.'

'And then you flew back?'

She hesitated. 'Eventually.'

'What does that mean?'

'Mother had another breakdown and we were—we had to stay there for several months.'

'And?'

'Then we came home, sold the house and moved to a smaller place.'

'Don't give me that!' he said with controlled violence. 'When we parted, your parents were living in a house worth a couple of million, with God knows how much in the bank! What went wrong? I want the truth!'

'Why?' she cried. 'So you can gloat?'

'Is that what you think of me?'

Not trusting herself to answer, she went on stroking the dog.

'I can see you feel very bitter about me,' Adam said in a low voice. 'But when I left you, I felt it was best for both of us if it was a clean break.'

'You were right.' With a supreme effort she raised her eyes to his. 'That's why I don't understand why you're suddenly interested in what happened to me after you left.'

'Call it curiosity.'

The word cut her like a knife. Cold, devoid of emotion; no love, no caring. Only curiosity.

Rising, she went to stand by the stone balustrade, turning slightly away from him to stare out at the swathe of green. Then, in a voice devoid of expression, she gave him a bald résumé of the last years. All she omitted were the frantic efforts she had made to contact him.

'Now that I've satisfied your curiosity,' she concluded, 'I hope you won't refer to the past again.'

'Only to say one thing.' He was so close, his breath was warm upon her ear. 'That I'd have done everything in my power to help you, if you had contacted me.'

'It never entered my head to do so,' she lied. 'When something is over, it's over.' Making her mouth curve in a smile, she swung round to him. 'That's what my nanny used to say.'

'So did the matron at the orphanage!' He returned her smile, though he was noticeably pale beneath his tan. 'But it's a maxim I've often had leave to doubt. You see I——'

'Hey, you two!' Claudia called. 'We're going in to lunch.'

'Coming,' Diana returned and, side-stepping Adam, sauntered down the terrace, head high, shoulders straight.

Just as Nanny would have liked.

CHAPTER SIXTEEN

LUNCH was a leisurely affair, with excellent wine and good food, though Diana was so heedful of Adam sitting directly opposite her that she might as well have been eating sawdust and drinking dishwater. He didn't appear to be affected in the same way, she noted sourly, which added to her irritation with Gordon for not telling her—until it was too late to cancel her date with him—that her ex-husband was going to be here today.

'If I had known it was going to be such a glorious weekend,' Lucy said as they returned to the terrace for coffee, 'I'd have asked you to stay the night. Come to think of it there's no reason why you can't. I can lend Claudia and Diana night things, and Simon has spare razors.'

'It's good of you to suggest it,' Adam responded, 'but Claudia and I have booked into Daleham Park.'

'We can't compete with *them*,' Lucy smiled. 'It's one of the best country hotels in Britain.' She glanced at Diana and Gordon. 'Any chance of persuading you two to stay on?'

Gordon glanced at Diana, who shook her head. 'Not today I'm afraid,' she murmured. 'I've made other arrangements for tomorrow.'

'Pity,' said Simon, passing the coffee. 'But maybe Adam and Claudia will join in tomorrow's hunt. You both ride, I assume?'

'I took it up a few years ago,' Adam said.

'But he has an excellent seat,' Claudia added.

'Well, we can lend you riding togs and——'

'Count me out,' Adam said easily. 'I'm against blood sports.'

'It's the one thing we don't agree on,' Claudia smiled. 'I keep telling him foxes are pests and need to be culled, but I can't convince him.'

'Tearing them to pieces isn't the way to do it,' Adam stated. 'It's about as humane as bashing baby seals on the head.'

'One can hardly compare the two,' Lucy protested. 'The fox has a chance of escaping—and you'd be surprised how many do.'

'Shall we change the subject?' he suggested mildly. 'We aren't going to agree, so it's purposeless arguing.'

'Don't you know women enjoying arguing?' This from Simon. 'Trouble is, they'll rarely admit they're wrong!'

'That's because we never are, darling!' his wife said. 'You should know that by now!'

It was three-thirty when they finally left the terrace for a tour of the house. Care and money had been lavished on it, and Diana could happily have moved in without altering a thing. All eight bedrooms had en-suite bathrooms, and no expense had been spared on modernising the enormous kitchen and domestic quarters.

'Mrs Graham is definitely not in the sale!' Lucy joked, placing a hand affectionately on the arm of the elderly cook. 'Simon says if it came to a choice, he'd rather part with *me*!'

Amid general laughter the group split up: the men returning to the terrace to talk business, the women strolling across the grounds, admiring the beautifully landscaped garden and various facilities. Apart from stables, there was a tennis court and glass-covered swimming-pool, complete with changing-rooms, sauna and fully equipped bar.

'If you fancy a swim, the water's heated,' Lucy told them.

'I'd adore one,' Diana said. She had drunk too much wine and felt heady. A dip might revive her. 'But I didn't bring a costume.'

'No problem. We have all sizes in a cupboard in one of the changing-rooms. How about you, Claudia?'

'I'm too lazy.'

'I'll keep you company, then. I do thirty lengths every morning, and that's my lot.'

Glad to be alone, Diana went in search of a costume. The swimsuits were all one-piece stretch cotton, and differed only in colour, and she chose a cornflower-blue one, the exact colour of her eyes. It clung like a second skin, showing off delicate curves that didn't have an ounce of superfluous fat. A pity Adam wasn't here to see her. Irritated by the errant thought, she padded to the pool and dived in.

She was an excellent swimmer and had always enjoyed a sensuous pleasure in the feel of water on her skin. She swam a length below the surface, then did a fast crawl back.

She was on her seventh lap when she noticed Adam watching her at the far end.

'Mind if I join you?' he called, and without waiting for a reply, disappeared to change.

He reappeared minutes later in the most minimal of briefs. It was six years since she had last seen him undressed, but his body was exactly as she remembered: wide shoulders, narrow waist, lean hips curving to hard muscled thighs.

Neatly diving in, he cleaved through it until he reached her.

'Everyone's taking a canter round the estate,' he informed her, treading water. 'Lucy's left trousers and a sweater in one of the guest rooms, in case you want to join them.'

'I'll stick to swimming,' Diana answered. 'It's more relaxing.'

'That's because you've had no competition! I'll race you to the far end.'

'I don't know if I have the strength. I've already done six lengths.'

'I'll give you half a length start.'

Accepting the challenge she struck out, but in spite of her strong, even strokes she was no match for his powerful crawl, and he swiftly overtook her.

'If I'd known you were so slow I'd have had a bet with you!' he teased as she reached his side.

'I'm out of practice,' she puffed defensively. 'I can't remember the last time I swam.'

'You can use the pool at my penthouse if you wish.'

She didn't comment, musing on Claudia's reaction if she accepted the offer. 'Have you made your decision about Kingsleigh?' she asked, switching the subject as she levered herself out to sit on the edge.

'Yes. I'm buying it.'

She tried to envisage Claudia living here. Her friend was a city girl and unlikely to relish being stuck in the heart of the countryside for any length of time.

'It isn't going to be *my* home,' Adam said, almost as if he had read her thoughts. 'It's for my company.'

'For meetings, you mean?'

'No, for the management; where they can unwind.' He hauled himself up next to her. 'I have a similar set-up in the States, and it works extremely well.'

'The ultimate executive perk!'

'If you like,' he shrugged. 'Stress is a big factor in causing illness, and anything one can do to alleviate it makes good sense.'

'Lucy and Simon will be surprised. They believe you want the house for yourself.'

'Do you see me as a country squire?' Adam asked bluntly.

'I don't know how I see you,' she admitted. 'You've changed.'

'Not so much that I'd relish being the odd man out. And that's what I'd be if I lived here. This is huntin', shootin' country, and not my scene. I'd like a country house, but I fancy the Cotswolds.'

'Parts of it are fabulous,' she said involuntarily.

'You can always be the housekeeper there!'

'I have an agency to run in London,' she said lightly. 'But when you do require a housekeeper, let me know. I have contacts with most of the good out-of-town agencies and I'll put in a good word for you.'

'That will make a change! You had none to say of me when we parted.'

Unwilling to enter a discussion that might give away her feelings for him, Diana slid back into the water. 'I'll do another lap and then change.'

'Me too.'

Predictably he finished ahead of her, and leaned forward to pull her out.

His touch set her heart racing, and she coloured as his eyes ranged over her. Her breasts firmed and tingled as if he had caressed them, her thighs quivered, and every part of her body became pulsatingly alive beneath his burnished brown gaze. As the heat of desire seared between her legs, she became afraid of her vulnerability to this man. Damn him for being so attractive! And damn him for reawakening emotions that could only cause her heartache.

Frightened in case he guessed what she was feeling, she went to draw away from him. But instead of releasing her, he tightened his grip and pulled her closer.

'Don't go,' he said throatily. 'You've wanted me to make love to you ever since you saw me again.'

'You're mad!'

'Mad to hold you close, to be inside you... We both want it, Di. Why pretend we don't?'

Before she could say 'because of Claudia', his warm mouth covered hers. 'My golden witch,' he whispered upon her lips. 'You cast a spell on me seven years ago and I can't break it.' The pressure of his mouth increased, so intent on assuagement that there was no time for tenderness.

Diana was powerless to resist him. How could she when she had longed for this for six empty years? Her lips parted to give him entry, and as he took it his arousal was instant. The leaping muscle between his legs pressed against the soft swell of her stomach, awakening her need, and her arms went round him to clasp him closer. Keeping his mouth fastened on hers, he lifted her up as easily as if she were a child and carried her swiftly towards the privacy of a changing-room.

As the door swung to behind them, he set her on her feet and flung a pile of fleecy towels to the floor, then, muttering deep in his throat, he drew her down on them.

They came together in a wonderful wild hunger, the feel of his nakedness, and his hard, pulsating erection inspiring her to a ferocity of excitement that was as new as it was wonderful. Everything that had gone before was but a prelude to this, and she knew that their past lovemaking counted for nothing. Their passion now was richer, more intense, kindled by the fire that sprang from their hard-won maturity.

They could not get enough of each other. Adam kissed and touched every part of her, stroking her breasts, sucking the nipples till they were tumescent as ripe red cherries, licking the gentle indent of her navel. Trembling with longing, Diana ran her hands along his spine, curved them over his firm buttocks and came to rest on the engorged muscle that throbbed against the wet triangle of blonde hair covering the pulsing bud of her femininity.

'God, I want you!' he cried, and moving on top of her, thrust deep.

Diana cried out with joy. Adam was inside her and the loneliness and emptiness of the past was over. Her muscles gripped his manhood so tightly that he groaned with pleasure and partially withdrew so that he could pierce her again, making gentle circling motions as he pulled slightly away and then plunged deeper, entering and withdrawing until she was in a frenzy of desire. The burning rod of his desire tormented her into losing control, and she raked her nails across his shoulders and pressed his buttocks harder so that he was closer to the soft swell of her stomach.

But still he held off, rearing and thrusting until his rhythm became hers and they moved as one, spinning together in a climactic explosion that had him bursting inside her, igniting her with the hot fluid of his life-giving sperm.

Languorously they drifted back to reason and lay close, her golden head pillowed on his shoulder, his hand curved around the fullness of her breast.

Distant voices brought them to their senses, and as she shifted in alarm, he gently levered himself off her.

'You're magic,' he said huskily. 'The only woman who satisfies me so completely.'

She was unable to echo the compliment for she had never been to bed with any man other than him. Yet if she admitted it, he was astute enough to guess she still cared about him. But wasn't that how he'd seen her recent surrender? Watching him rise and stand in naked magnificence in front of her, with no trace of embarrassment visible, though his continued arousal was all too evident, she knew that for a man the act of love did not necessarily mean love, but the appeasement of desire.

And that was all the past half-hour had meant to him. To imagine otherwise was foolish. He had wanted her and he had taken her. Indeed she had made it easy for him. But she had no regrets. Well, perhaps one: that her monthly cycle had just finished and there was no chance of becoming pregnant. Tears misted her eyes. How she would have revelled in having his child, even though it would have meant leaving London—possibly even going abroad to live—to keep it secret from him.

'You aren't angry with me, are you?' he asked softly.

'I have no right to be. I didn't try to stop you.'

'I'm not sure you'd have succeeded. You were always able to make me lose my head—and you still can.'

'I can say the same about you.' She forced a smile. 'We sound like a couple of characters from a Noel Coward play!'

'So we do. And the curtain's come down for intermission.'

What a nerve he had! Did he think she'd allow another curtain-raiser? Remembering Claudia, she could barely hide her disgust of him—and herself too, come to that.

'Not intermission,' she said, avoiding his eyes as she draped her nudity with a towel and rose gracefully to her feet. 'That was the last act, Adam. The play has ended.'

'There's always tomorrow.'

At this, she *did* look at him, noting that his bantering tone didn't go with his tightly clenched jaw. 'What are you trying to prove? That we're sexually compatible? We always were, even up to the night you walked out! But as we both know, one can't build anything lasting on sex alone.'

With a supreme effort she walked past him. Her towel brushed the side of his arm but she made no move to avoid the contact, knowing that to show indifference to his closeness was the best way of endorsing what she had said.

Not until she was alone in an adjacent room did her nerves get the better of her and, trembling like a leaf, she sank on to a bench. She didn't know how long she remained there, but Adam had long since returned to the house before she summoned the strength to dress and do the same.

Did she look like a woman recently racked by passion? Who had soared to the stars? True, the redness of her mouth owed nothing to lipstick, nor the glow of her skin to rouge, though both could be the result of nothing more innocuous than a strenuous swim! Luckily, no prying eyes were able to see the faint bruising round her nipples caused by Adam's frenzied sucking, nor the swollen bud between her thighs that still throbbed with remembered ecstasy.

Drawing a deep breath, she sauntered on to the terrace, where tea was being served.

'Enjoyed your swim?' Claudia asked. She was sitting close to Adam on the hammock, one slender thigh touching his muscled one.

'It was great, but I'm absolutely exhausted. I should join a health club to get fit.'

'We run several for our employees,' Adam informed her. 'Gordon can give you the name of one nearest to you.'

'Don't take me so literally!' Diana gave a light laugh. 'I loathe enforced exercise.'

The conversation turned to health care in general, and after a while Adam rose and drew Claudia to her feet.

'We must be making a move,' he said to Lucy and Simon. 'I don't want to lose our booking.'

His glance strayed momentarily to Diana, but he did not single her out for a special goodbye.

Gordon rose too, but Lucy shook her head at him. 'We're not letting you and Diana rush off too. Supper's already arranged.'

Diana hid her chagrin, not relishing making small talk when all she wanted was to be alone and relive what had happened in the pool house. Yet wasn't it better to forget it? She almost laughed aloud, knowing that Adam was imprinted on her psyche, and that as long as breath was in her body, she would not forget the exquisite pleasure of being part of him. What price her future with another man now? she wondered bleakly, and knew it would be a long while—if ever—before she could contemplate it.

It was past midnight when Gordon deposited her at the door of the Grosvenor Square apartment.

'Thanks for a wonderful day,' she said.

'It isn't finished yet.' Catching her by the waist, he drew her close.

Making herself relax, she let him kiss her, hoping that his touch would give perspective to her feelings for Adam. But all it did was heighten them, making it impossible for her to simulate a response.

Aware of it, he let her go. 'You're tired.'

'Very,' she agreed, not wishing to hurt him.

'May I see you next week? Wednesday and the weekend?'

'It depends when I'm moving. I want to leave here as soon as possible.'

'Claudia being difficult?'

'Not really. But it *is* embarrassing—for both of us. Call me on Tuesday and I should know when I'm free.'

He looked as if he wanted to argue, but deciding against it, he touched his hand to her cheek and left.

Dejectedly she went into the apartment, trying not to picture Adam and Claudia, and that damn black lace nightgown! He couldn't be making love to her. Not to-

night; not when a few hours 'ago he had taken herself
with such intensity.

Yet passion came and went, and without love was
simply a momentary gratification. It hurt deeply to admit
that this was all she meant to him, but to believe
otherwise was wishful thinking.

'No!' she cried aloud. 'Six years is long enough. I
won't go on hoping. I won't!'

Perhaps if she said it forcefully enough, she might believe it.

CHAPTER SEVENTEEN

FORTUNATELY most of Sunday was taken up viewing furnished rooms, and by the end of the day Diana knew she couldn't bear to live in a bedsitter. And why should she when she was banking a healthy profit each week from the agency? It was stupid not to save a little less and rent an empty apartment that she could furnish and make into a comfortable home. After the emotional battering she had taken, it was likely to be her base for years to come! First thing tomorrow she'd have her secretary ring round to see what was on the market.

This decided, she took herself to a film. It was one she wanted to see, but she was so preoccupied thinking of Claudia and Adam that it was impossible to concentrate on it. Besides, she was anxious to be in bed before her friend returned. It would at least spare her the necessity of listening to the marvellous time Claudia had had!

But luck was against her, for as she let herself into the hall, the American girl called to her from the bedroom. Pasting a light-hearted expression on her face, Diana went in to see her.

Claudia was in bed, glamorous in the silk and lace nightgown she had bought for her weekend away. Her hair was a gleaming red nimbus round her head, and her eyes were glowing bright as lamps. No lovelorn girl here, returning from a disappointing weekend, Diana thought bleakly.

'Been out with Gordon?' came the question.

'No. I took myself to the cinema. He wanted to see me but I cried off.'

'Why? He fancies you, and from what Adam's told me, he's a great catch.' Claudia patted the side of her bed. 'Come and chat for a few moments. I'm too strung up to sleep.'

Hiding her reluctance, Diana did as she was told. 'Only for a few minutes, though. I'm knocked out. I've been rushing round all day looking at bedsits, but they were so grotty I've decided to rent something better.'

'There's no rush for you to go—not any longer.' Claudia gave a shamefaced smile. 'I asked you to leave because I was jealous that you'd been married to Adam, and I wasn't sure how he felt about you. But after this weekend, I've no more worries.' She lay back against the pillows. 'I've never known him so loving and tender. Saturday night we made it three times, and yesterday we stayed in bed until we left to drive home!'

Nausea gripped Diana, and it was agony to stay in the room. She felt dirty, betrayed, and furiously angry for believing, deep in her heart, that Adam's taking of her yesterday had meant more to him than sexual gratification. Just showed how naïve she still was, crediting him with virtues he didn't possess, with motives unfounded on reality. He had made love to her because she had been like a bitch in heat and he had scented that she wanted him. It had been nothing other than an ego trip.

'He said no woman has ever satisfied him as I do,' Claudia murmured dreamily, 'and when he said that, all my jealousy of you vanished.'

Diana tasted the bitterness of gall. Twenty-four hours ago he had used the same words to her. It seemed there was no limit to his betrayal.

'Don't believe everything a man says to you,' she commented drily. 'It's what he does that counts.'

Claudia gave a sympathetic murmur. 'I don't expect you to say otherwise. Your marriage didn't work out, and naturally you're bitter.'

Diana rose. It was pointless reminding Claudia that until she had discovered her Adam and Diana's were one and the same, she had vehemently laid all the blame for the broken marriage at *his* door.

'I hope things work out for you,' she said instead, hoping she sounded sincere.

'They already have,' Claudia beamed. 'Look!' She held up her left hand, which had been partially hidden beneath the duvet. On the third finger a huge diamond sparkled. 'Adam gave it to me this morning,' she said huskily. 'Isn't it sensational?'

Diana nodded dumbly. Even if she had wanted to, she couldn't have spoken.

'I'm walking on cloud nine,' her friend went on. 'It's a dream come true. Adam is everything I've ever wanted.'

I thought the same once, Diana reflected when she was alone at last, and wished with every beat of her heart that she hadn't met Claudia again; hadn't seen Adam and reawakened her love for him. But it was a doomed love, and she would not waste her life in regrets.

Next morning, hollow-eyed but clear-thinking, she headed for her office instead of the penthouse, afraid that if she saw him she'd lose her temper and, in doing so, expose her love. Eventually she would be able to meet him with equanimity, but not while her emotions were this raw.

As she expected, he telephoned at nine to find out where she was, and Kathy answered as instructed.

'There was an emergency in the office and Miss Farrow had to attend to it. She's extremely sorry and hopes to be at the apartment later today.'

As Kathy replaced the receiver, she flung her employer a puzzled frown. 'Any reason for playing hard to get?'

'Yes, but it's personal.'

'Well, he said for you to contact him as soon as you're free. It's urgent.'

Diana nodded, but had no intention of doing so. She was meeting Marla—her best daily help—at the apartment this afternoon, having changed the girl's itinerary so she could take over the job. Adam was an important client and could damage her agency's reputation if she let him down, though on a personal level she'd have enjoyed seeing him swamped by dust, rotting food and dirty linen!

What would happen when he married? she wondered later that day as she walked briskly through the magnificent rooms with Marla. It was difficult envisaging Claudia being content with a single daily.

A picture of the attic room she and Adam had shared in Kilburn flashed before her eyes. He had been mad as a pole cat when he had discovered she was sending his shirts to a hand laundry, though she had paid for it with her money. He had even objected to her buying ready prepared food from Marks and Spencer, and when she had accepted a tiny pot of caviare from her parents, he had blown his top. Today a valet took care of his linen, and he was unlikely to object if Claudia bought those damned fish eggs by the ton!

'Shall I start cleaning up now, Miss Farrow?' Marla cut into her thoughts.

'No, thanks, you've already worked a full day.'

'So have you!'

'The penalty of being the boss! No, you start tomorrow.'

When Marla had gone, Diana tidied the rooms Adam had used. She noted he was still neat: the clothes he had used during the weekend placed in a pile ready for the valet who came three times a week, the wet towels in the bathroom carefully hung on the heated rails to dry, a coffee-cup set in the sink.

She was rinsing the cup and resisting the urge to place the rim to her mouth, where Adam's lips had rested, when the telephone rang. She swung round to answer it, then stopped. It was bound to be Adam and she didn't want to talk to him. Yet she longed to hear his voice, and she raced into his study, where the answering machine came on automatically after five rings.

But the voice she heard was Gordon's, and she snatched up the receiver.

'Sorry, Gordon, I was cleaning the shower and didn't get to the phone in time.'

'No sweat. I was merely checking to see if you'd found a place to live, yesterday.'

'No. But I found where I *don't* want to live.' She was halfway through explaining when he interrupted her.

'It won't be easy finding something you like at a price you can afford. And to give you breathing space, you can move into the mews cottage behind my house in Sussex Square. The tenants left a few days ago, and it will be ideal for you. It's fully furnished and waiting to be occupied.'

'What's the rent?' she asked hesitantly, uncertain if living in proximity to him was a good idea.

'Eighty pounds a week.'

'It's far too low.'

'It's a very small cottage—and I don't want to make a profit out of you. Accept it gracefully, Diana.'

Jane would have said the same, and she sighed. 'It sounds too good to be true.'

'It's settled, then. Have dinner with me tonight and you can look it over.'

'Blackmailer!'

'I assume that means yes,' he chuckled. 'I'll collect you at eight.'

As she set down the receiver, it rang again, and without thinking she picked it up, exasperated with herself when she heard Adam speak.

'Why haven't you called me?' he demanded. 'I left messages at Grosvenor Square, and with your secretary.'

'I had business matters to attend to,' she replied.

'Anything wrong?'

'Nothing I can't handle.'

'Are you sure? You sound strange.'

'I'm busy, that's why.'

'Busy or not, we have to talk.'

'What about?'

'Don't give me that!'

Diana shifted the receiver from one sweating palm to the other. 'So talk.'

'Face to face.' His voice faded momentarily. 'Damn! I've a call from my Chicago office I have to take. I'll speak to you later.'

Returning to the kitchen, she pondered on his abrupt change of tactics. One moment his need to see her was urgent, the next he'd used a hackneyed excuse as a delaying tactic. Was it because he needed time to work out a way of excusing his behaviour? Of ensuring she didn't tell his future wife he had made love to his last one twenty-four hours ago? His perfidy sickened her and she was shaking so much that the cutlery she was putting away in the drawer fell from her hands. Shovelling it in, she reached for her coat and walked out.

Vision blinded by tears, she went down to the garage and her car. Switching on the engine, she slowly backed out of the parking bay, stopping abruptly as a dark grey Bentley swooped across her path with a sharp squeal of brakes, blocking her in. Oh no! Now she knew why Adam had said he had to take another call!

In three strides he was at her door, black-haired, dark-suited, grim-faced. 'I guessed you'd cut and run. Get out. We'll talk upstairs.'

'I'd rather talk here.'

'Your car or mine?'

'Mine,' she replied, preferring the advantage of home ground, but instantly regretting it as he squeezed his long length into the front passenger seat, and she realised how close he was to her.

'Why are you avoiding me?' he asked. 'And don't lie and say you aren't, because I've had enough of the run-around.'

He'd had enough of the run-around! Her blood boiled with indignation.

'I wasn't running away from you, nor do I know what we have to talk over.'

'Us,' he said succinctly. 'You and me.'

'There *is* no you and me. There's you and Claudia.'

'Ahh,' he sighed. 'I had a feeling she was at the bottom of it.'

'Clever of you,' she said bitterly. 'But don't worry. I won't tell her, or blackmail you for my silence. What happened at the pool house wasn't important, and I've forgotten it.'

Dark brown eyes narrowed to slits, and his mouth clamped into a thin line. 'Have you?'

'Yes. It isn't anything I care to remember.' Stonily she regarded him. 'You made love to me to prove you still had power over me. You wanted to humble me, to pay me back for putting my parents before you... For not loving you enough. Well, where was *your* love when I needed it?' The words tumbled from her as all the old resentments resurfaced. 'Where was your love when my father was ill, when he died, when we lost everything? You didn't phone, didn't write, didn't give a damn!'

'I didn't know about it. I was already in the States.'

'My father's company was as well known in America as here,' she said flatly. 'When it collapsed it made news in every national paper over there. You knew, but you didn't care. You were a selfish, self-centred swine then, and in spite of your money and success, you still are! Nothing has changed.'

'Too true. You've always liked thinking the worst of me.'

'Give me one reason why I shouldn't!'

'And spoil your image of me?' He laughed: a cold, raucous sound. 'If you didn't have me to hate, you'd fall apart! It was hating me that kept you going all these years; gave you the strength to cope with your mother and your poverty.'

There was a lot of truth in what he said, and she admitted it. 'But I don't have to cope with my mother or poverty any longer,' she added, 'so I can finally forget you.'

'You really despise me, don't you?' he said quietly.

'Not now. You aren't the man I thought you were, Adam. So how can I despise what doesn't exist? I hope you'll be happy with Claudia. She told me last night about your engagement.'

He leaned forward menacingly. 'And you assumed I was scared you might try blackmailing me?'

'Well, you were so insistent on seeing me...'

'You misunderstood my reason.' His mouth curved in an unpleasant smile. 'It wouldn't harm things between Claudia and myself if you *did* tell her. Quite the contrary.'

'Really?' Diana shot him a scornful glance.

'Sure.' He stepped from the car, and spoke through the open window. 'Asking her to marry me on Sunday, when I'd had *you* on Saturday, should show her how I rate you!'

Pain rendered speech impossible, and mutely she watched him climb into the Bentley and reverse it so she could drive out. Only as she came abreast of him did she find her voice again.

'Another housekeeper will be taking over from me. She's the best one we have. I'm also leaving Grosvenor Square tomorrow, so you won't be embarrassed by my presence.'

'It never bothered me.' His tone was laconic. 'You found a place quickly.'

'Courtesy of Gordon. I'm moving into his mews cottage.'

'Convenient for you.'

'Don't be a dog in the manger, darling.' Diana spoke in her most upper-class tone. 'You aren't the only one who's going to live happily ever after.'

'I hope we'll both be luckier second time around.'

'I'm sure *I* shall. Gordon comes from the same background and we have much more in common.'

Adam unexpectedly grinned, looking like the brash young man she had met that fateful Sunday at the Tate Gallery. 'Let's hope he doesn't treat you like a lady when you're in the sack with him! He won't keep you happy that way.'

'I can always show him what will,' she purred. 'That's one thing I'll always thank you for. You were a marvellous teacher!'

Upon which she drove smartly away, glad she had had the last word, and infinitely glad he could not see the tears pouring down her cheeks.

CHAPTER EIGHTEEN

IN AN effort to forget Adam, Diana flung herself into work, seeing it as the best panacea.

Gordon helped too, openly showing his eagerness to spend as much time with her as she would allow him.

The cottage she was renting from him had been her salvation, and she dreaded to think how she would have survived the trauma of Adam's impending marriage had she been living in a soulless bedsitter. Not only was her temporary home beautifully furnished, but larger than he had led her to believe, and it even had a tiny patio on which the sun shone all day.

In the two months of living there, she had made an effort to find outside interests, and this had included making new friends, apart from catching up with all her old ones.

'I'm delighted you're leading a full life again,' Jane commented one day over lunch at Langan's. She had recently become engaged to the son of a city bigwig, and was intent on marrying off her friend too. 'The next step for you is marriage. Gordon's a——'

'I don't love him,' Diana cut in.

'So what? You adored Adam, and where did it get you?' Jane tossed her head, her pertly pretty face unusually serious. 'You're still carrying the torch for him, aren't you?'

'Yes.' Diana drew a deep breath. 'Yes, I am. I loathe myself for it but I can't get over him.'

She lapsed into silence. A month after their stormy scene in the garage, Adam had returned to America, shortly followed by Claudia. He came to London rarely, and only stayed a few days. Having recruited a team of bright young executives to run his English venture, he had put Gordon in charge of the entire British operation.

It was Gordon who had unexpectedly asked her to engage the staff for Kingsleigh, the country house that was being turned into a retreat for their employees, and when she demurred, had informed her he was doing it on Adam's instructions.

'You astonish me,' she had commented. 'We didn't part friends, you know.'

'So I gathered. But he was very specific, none the less. Said you knew your business—he's delighted with Marla incidentally—and trusts your judgement. The house should be ready for occupation in a couple of months, so you'd better get cracking.'

It had not been an easy task, but the commission was going to be lucrative, for she had to engage a full staff of five, plus gardeners to take care of the extensive grounds. She had advertised in local Wiltshire papers, and after a few false starts, found the people she required.

A week ago, with most of the interior décor finished, Mr and Mrs Marshall, the butler-handyman and cook-housekeeper, had moved in to supervise the final details. They had written to ask when she was coming to spend a weekend with them and test out the staffing arrangements, but she had pleaded work, doubting whether she had the courage to return to a house that held memories she longed to forget.

'If you can't forget Adam,' Jane said into the silence, 'then you should try to patch things up with him. Until he marries Claudia, nothing is hopeless.'

'How can you even suggest it?' Diana was astonished. Jane knew everything that had happened that Saturday

in Wiltshire, as well as her last stormy meeting with him.
'You can't be serious.'

'I am. I've been giving it a lot of thought lately, and
I'm not convinced he made love to you to prove he still
had power over you. He's too confident a man to need
that sort of ego-boost. I think he fancied you like mad
and couldn't resist you.'

'You're making him more of a swine, not less! You're
forgetting he was Claudia's lover as well, and he made
love to her again a few hours after he——'

'Because you made it clear you despised him! If you
hadn't, he might have behaved differently.'

'If... might... It's all pie in the sky. I can only judge
him on his actions.'

'My point exactly!' Jane was triumphant. 'Take this
engagement of his. I think he asked Claudia to marry
him just to spite you. If he genuinely wanted her, he'd
have married her by now. How long has he been
engaged?'

'Three months.'

'And he still hasn't tied the knot. I bet it isn't because
she's holding back. If——'

'No more, Jane,' Diana said wearily. 'It's not worth
discussing.'

'It *is* if you love him. He's ruining things between you
and Gordon, and he'll do the same with any other man
you meet. Don't let pride stop you from doing what your
heart dictates. Call Adam and tell him you love him,
then see what he does.'

'Laughs,' Diana retorted.

'OK. If that's how he reacts, you'll know you're well
rid of him. But if he doesn't... Take a chance, Diana,
it's worth it if you can get back together.'

Jane's advice lingered in her mind, and several times
during the week she almost dialled his office in Chicago.
But pride stopped her. Pride, and the knowledge that

this was a road she had travelled before. From their very first meeting she had pursued *him*, never the other way round. Even when she had returned to London, after her father's death, she had done everything possible to contact him, willing to continue their marriage in spite of everything. But his instructions to his lawyers had shown how unbending he was. Surely she didn't need another put-down?

If Adam wanted her, let *him* make the first move.

Three days later, a call from Claudia put paid to any hope of this.

'Diana, honey, how *are* you?' she gushed in her over-the-top manner. Then typically, didn't wait for a reply. 'It's months since we spoke, and I've reams to tell you. I'm getting married in two weeks' time. Isn't it great?'

'Great,' Diana echoed, wondering what one gave to an ex-husband and his new bride. A record of 'Love's More Wonderful the Second Time Around' perhaps, or a silver bowl filled with sour grapes!

'How are things with you and Gordon?' Claudia enquired.

'We're still dating.'

'You should pull in the line. He's too good a catch to let slip!' Claudia laughed at her own joke. 'I wish you could see my wedding dress. Christian Lacroix is making it, and it has fifty metres of chiffon! We're honeymooning in Tahiti,' she chatted on. 'I've always thought it the most romantic place in the world—don't you?'

'Oh, yes.' It was certainly more romantic than Adam's first honeymoon in Kilburn!

'We'll be in London towards the end of July,' Claudia continued, 'and we must get together then.'

Diana mumbled something appropriate, relieved when the call ended. She finally had her answer, and Jane would have no more reason to nag her. All she had to do now, was to put Adam out of her mind. Some hope!

She hadn't managed it during the years since their divorce, and there was no reason to suppose it was going to be easier now.

Yet she was nothing if not a fighter, and the last few years had honed it to perfection. Her ever-expanding business stopped her thinking of Adam during the day, and in the hope of banishing him from the nights she began leading a hectic social life: dining out constantly, and dancing at Annabel's and Tramps until the early hours of the morning, when she would fall into bed too exhausted to think.

'Why such frenetic activity?' Gordon questioned over dinner at Mosimann's one evening.

Diana had not seen him for more than a week. He had been touring the company's out-of-town stores and, because she did not want to give him false hopes, she had dated other men.

'I'm making up for lost time,' she responded lightly.

'Is there a particular reason behind it?'

Although his tone gave nothing away, she felt he had guessed that Adam's imminent wedding was distressing her. For an instant she was mortified, then was unexpectedly relieved she could at last be truthful with him. But only up to a point. Adam was his employer and, as such, would not welcome Gordon knowing the intimate details of his life.

'I thought I'd got over Adam,' she confessed huskily, 'but when I saw him again I realised I hadn't. I knew he and Claudia were having an affair, but I suppose I hoped... Anyway, events proved me wrong. They're getting married a week today, as you know.'

'I didn't.'

'Oh.' Awkwardly she looked away. 'Claudia didn't say it was a secret, and I assumed you knew.'

Gordon shook his head. 'Adam's always kept his private life private. If he didn't, the media wouldn't give him any peace. He's probably getting married in some out-of-the-way place that they'll never find.'

Which wouldn't please Claudia, in her fifty metres of chiffon! Diana thought bitchily, and was overtaken by such a wave of jealousy that she could have screamed.

'I'm glad he's taking the plunge,' Gordon continued. 'It should help you to forget him.'

'Jane says the same.'

'Great minds think alike!' He leaned across the table and rested his hand on hers. 'Time's a great healer. It's a cliché but it's true.'

'You're sweet,' she said, meaning it. 'I'd much rather be in love with you.'

'I endorse that!' A smile lit his narrow face. 'And to be honest, with Adam out of the way, you've given me new reason to hope.'

'You won't mention it to anyone, will you?' she asked anxiously.

'What? That my hopes are rising like a rocket to the moon?'

'No, silly.' She softened her words with a smile. 'That Adam's getting married.'

'What marriage?' he asked with total innocence.

Satisfied, Diana picked up her wine glass and drained it.

The day of Adam's wedding, she made sure she had a back-breaking schedule, though it did not prevent her continuously glancing at her watch, seeing the seconds turn into minutes, the minutes into hours. If she knew the time of the ceremony she could drink a toast to it, she thought wryly, convinced Jane and Gordon were right, and that once Adam was Claudia's husband, she would be free of him.

Predictably, Gordon telephoned and asked her to have dinner with him, but she refused.

'Why? Do you plan on wallowing in an evening of misery?' he asked bluntly.

'Don't harangue me. I'm feeling fragile.'

'Sorry.' He cleared his throat. 'I—er—I heard from Adam last night.'

Diana felt as if she had been kicked in the stomach. 'Did he——?'

'Not a word. Only that he's taking a month off, as of today, and wants me to stand in for him in Chicago. I'm flying there tomorrow.'

'I'll miss you.'

'Good.' He hesitated. 'I'll be in touch. Take care.'

Although Diana expected to spend the evening wallowing in misery, she was surprised to find she wasn't able to shed a tear. It was as if she were numb. She couldn't even envisage Claudia in Adam's arms. All she saw was her friend floating on a cloud of chiffon! Perhaps humour would prove to be the best way of eradicating Adam.

The following morning Mrs Marshall, the housekeeper she had engaged for Kingsleigh, contacted her at the office to say that next Tuesday the first group of employees would be arriving to spend a week there.

'The house is looking beautiful, Miss Farrow, and we're all raring to go. In fact we hope you'll come down this weekend and give us a chance to have a dry run.'

Diana hesitated. Perhaps returning to Kingsleigh and swimming in the pool and using the changing-room would exorcise memories that were still haunting her. Certainly staying away hadn't helped them to fade.

'You've talked me into it, Mrs Marshall. Expect me Saturday lunchtime.'

'Can't you make it dinner on Friday? Then you'd have two clear days.'

'Very well. Friday it shall be.'

CHAPTER NINETEEN

KINGSLEIGH looked lovelier than Diana had remembered, as she bowled down the drive late Friday afternoon and parked her car below the sweeping stone steps. Standing clear and bold against the pale blue spring sky, its magnificence took her breath away.

Stuart Marshall, an athletic-looking, well-preserved fifty, opened the front door to her and escorted her to her room, where tea and biscuits awaited her.

'When you've had a rest, I'll show you around,' he said.

'I can't wait to see everything. I'll be downstairs in fifteen minutes.'

She was as good as her word, and together they inspected the reception rooms and some of the bedrooms. The designers had followed their brief to the letter, and despite numerous alterations to increase the sleeping capacity, and the addition of a leisure complex containing squash courts, and a billiard room, Kingsleigh still had the feel of a private country home.

The pool and changing-rooms had been left untouched, and peeping hurriedly into them, she marvelled that she felt no emotion. Was she numb from grief, she asked herself, or finally coming to terms with the inevitable?

Her last stop was the kitchen, where Mrs Marshall welcomed her, plump and pretty and proud to show off the array of electrical equipment and special ovens.

'Dinner's at eight-thirty, Miss Farrow, and Stuart will serve drinks in the drawing-room half an hour before.'

'That rule applies only to company employees,' her husband corrected, then smiled at Diana. 'The drinks cabinet is open so please help yourself.'

'Don't spoil me too much, or you might not get rid of me on Monday morning!'

'We don't see that as a threat!' Mrs Marshall laughed, and Diana was warmed by the comment as she returned to her room for a rest.

Surveying herself in the mirror-fronted wardrobe before going down to dinner, she was pleased she had recently had her hair restyled, going to a hairdresser who was the current darling of *Harper's*. He had enthused over its golden colour, and had decided against cutting it short, contenting himself with shaping it so that the smooth waves she had cultivated these past few years returned to the bubbly curls of her teens. Her initial shock had quickly turned to pleasure when she found herself getting openly admiring glances from every male she met, and it had done wonders for her self-confidence.

As she went down the sweeping staircase she was sorry she hadn't packed a long dress, for the elegant hall seemed to demand the rustle of satin. Still, her emerald linen dress was a good foil for the panelling, besides giving her skin the iridescent glow of a pearl.

Entering the drawing-room she experienced a fleeting sadness, for the pastel beauty of the room, with its peach and almond-green squashy sofas and armchairs, its bowls of fragrant flowers, and the log fire crackling in the huge grate to take the chill from the spring evening, called out for the presence of a man. Not just any man, but a special one. Adam.

Damn, damn, damn! She had vowed to stop thinking of him, yet the moment she felt romantic, she could think of no one else. She headed for the drinks cabinet, stopping in surprise as she saw an opened jeroboam of Louis Roederer nestling invitingly in an ice bucket on a low table in front of the sofa nearest the fire. Beside it was a small crystal bowl heaped with tiny gleaming fish eggs, and a plate of blinis—tiny buckwheat pancakes.

Heavens! Vintage champagne and caviare! The Marshalls had said they wanted her to feel at home, but this was ridiculous. She hoped Adam didn't scrutinise the Kingsleigh expense accounts. But that was even more ridiculous. He was far too high-powered to bother with such things.

Lifting out the bottle, she filled a narrow fluted glass.

'Would you care to pour one for me?' a deep male voice requested, and with a startled gasp she swung round.

'Adam!' Her heart pounded so loudly in her ears that she wasn't sure she had spoken his name aloud. What was he doing here? He should be in Tahiti with Claudia— unless she was here too? 'You—you're the last person I expected to see.'

'Kingsleigh *does* belong to me.'

'I know, but I——' She broke off, trying to gather her scattered wits. 'I assumed you and Claudia were in Tahiti.'

'As far as I know she *is* there.' Closing the double doors behind him, he came further into the room. 'But I doubt whether her husband would take kindly to my joining them.'

Diana stared at him in bewilderment. 'But *you're* her husband.'

Adam's brows drew together in a frown, darkening eyes from which the amber lights were gone, as though dimmed by the sombreness of his thoughts. He looked far from well. Deep lines were incised either side of his mouth, and there were heavy shadows on his lids and punched hollows beneath his cheekbones. Hardly the glowing face of a bridegroom, she thought, though it gave him a sensual, brooding quality that made her weak at the knees.

'Who told you?' he asked abruptly.

'Claudia. She called me a few weeks ago to say she was marrying you on the sixteenth and going to Tahiti on her honeymoon.'

'Well, she did get married on the sixteenth, and I understand she's honeymooning in Tahiti. I'm not speaking from first-hand knowledge, though. I read it in the papers.'

Diana tried to recall exactly what Claudia had said. Come to think of it, she had never mentioned Adam by name, nor had she seen fit to admit they were no longer engaged; omissions that must have been deliberate. But why had she wanted to give the impression she was marrying him?

'I haven't seen Claudia since I returned to the States,' Adam stated abruptly, moving forward to take the bottle from her hand.

Diana put some distance between them, using the pretext of sitting down. 'I wasn't aware you'd broken your engagement.'

'I didn't.'

She reddened. 'I'm sorry.'

'There's no reason to be. I wasn't engaged to her in the first place.'

'Oh?' Diana's heart missed a beat. 'What about the engagement ring you gave her?'

'I gave her a ring,' he corrected, 'but it wasn't an engagement one, and I never asked her to marry me.' With jerky movements, at variance with his calm voice, he poured himself a glass of champagne and took an armchair directly opposite Diana. 'I don't deny that at one stage I considered asking her to marry me, but after seeing you again I had too many doubts. Doubts which became a certainty after you and I made love that Saturday afternoon.'

Diana slammed down her glass on the table beside her. 'Not so much of a certainty that it stopped you making love to Claudia that same evening!'

'Is that what you think?' In three strides he was in front of her. 'Look at me, dammit!' He waited until she did. 'Do you honestly think that after what we shared that Saturday, I made love to another woman? I'm no saint, lord knows, and I'm not saying I was celibate the years we were apart, but once I saw you again I was no good to any other woman.'

Colour stained Diana's cheeks and her eyes slid away from the dark brown ones impaling her. 'From the frequency with which you saw Claudia, I didn't get that impression,' she said stiffly. 'Nor from the things she said.'

'You weren't in my bedroom,' he retorted. 'And we both now know what a bloody liar she is!'

Diana couldn't contradict this, yet she was still too bewildered to accept what Adam was saying.

'I can't begin to guess what that bitch told you,' he went on hoarsely. 'But one thing you have to believe: from the moment I admitted to myself that I hadn't got over you, that I wanted another chance with you, I never touched her. Never touched any woman!'

'Then why did you stay with Claudia in that country hotel? And what about the ring you gave her? I know you're wealthy, but even *you* can't call it a trinket!'

'It was a peace offering.' A tinge of pink rose in his face. 'A guilt offering, to be honest. As for staying in the hotel...' He shook his head. 'Claudia made the booking herself, and at the time I went along with it because I didn't want to quarrel with her.'

'Why not?'

Adam's lower lip jutted forward, giving him the look of a little boy caught being naughty. 'I was trying to make you jealous. You'd made it plain you despised me, yet I had a gut feeling you didn't, and I figured that if I went on seeing Claudia and she kept talking about me, you'd acknowledge how you felt. I had no idea she was making you believe I was still her lover. Stupid of me,' he confessed rawly, 'but where you're concerned I've always been stupid. That Saturday, when we left here, I said we should cancel our hotel booking and return to London. I told her I was still in love with you and was going to do everything in my power to get you back. She took it remarkably well—said she'd thought as much—and hoped I'd succeed. Then she floored me by asking if we could still stay the night in the hotel—said it would give her happy memories of our parting. I felt such a swine for using her the way I had, that I couldn't say no. But we had separate rooms and I never touched her.'

Remembering everything Claudia had said about that weekend, Diana found it incredible that a girl she had considered her friend should have acted so wickedly. However much Claudia had loved Adam and wanted to keep him, her duplicity was unforgivable. Had she genuinely cared for him she would have wanted his happiness, not set out to destroy it. Yet even to the last, she had been venomous. Thinking how much Claudia must have hated her to have acted this way, she shivered.

'That day in the garage—when I accused you of being engaged to her,' she said shakily, 'why didn't you tell me the truth then?'

'Pride,' he answered shortly. 'I was furious with you for your lack of trust. I felt that no matter what I said, you'd always doubt me, so I decided to return to the States.'

Another question rose in her mind. It had been there for years, a canker eating into her, and she had to know the answer.

'When you walked out on me years ago, why did you disappear without a trace? Didn't you care what happened to me?'

Anguish twisted his face, and several seconds ticked away before he spoke. 'When you went on the cruise with your parents, I was jealous and hurt. It made me realise I was years away from giving you the good things in life, and——'

'I didn't go with them for that reason!' she cried. 'I went because they needed me.'

'I see that now, but at the time I was too jealous of their hold on you to be logical. That's why I disappeared, refused to have any contact with you. I knew that unless I did, I'd weaken.'

'Did you think I'd quickly get over you and marry again?'

'Yes.'

'I'm amazed you weren't curious to know if your judgement of me was correct,' she said bitterly. 'Think how it would have justified your actions if you'd found out that as soon as we were divorced I had married one of the rich young men you so patently disliked!'

'I couldn't bear to know,' he said huskily. 'I flung myself into work and for years never thought of anything else. I wouldn't let myself think of you . . .'

His voice was so soft that she had to strain to hear it, and she knew the effort it was costing him to bare his soul to her.

'It wasn't until I met Claudia and began to wonder if I could rebuild my life with another woman, that I knew I had to see you first; had to make sure I could bury your ghost. So I gave myself a legitimate business reason for coming back to England. That way, if you were happily married, I could pretend it didn't matter to me. You see, even then I wasn't being honest with myself. But once I saw you, I was forced to face the truth.'

'Which was?'

'That you are the only woman I will ever love. I'll never forgive myself for the misery I caused you,' he went on in a cracked voice. 'Marry me, Di. Let me spend the rest of my life making it up to you.'

'No.'

Adam stepped back from her, his skin taking on a greyish tinge. 'I—I can't say I blame you. After what I did, I——'

'No, Adam, you don't understand.' She jumped up and reached out to touch his arm. 'I don't want you thinking you have to atone for the past. What's done is done. Besides, I wasn't blameless. I was young and silly and didn't make allowances for——'

'Don't make it easy for me,' he cut in, pulling her close and pressing her body against his. 'I *should* have found out how your father was; I should never have disappeared the way I did. When I think of what you went through, all you suffered...'

His voice broke and he buried his head against the side of her neck. Diana felt his tears on her skin, and they were her undoing. With a muffled cry, she stroked his hair.

'Adam, don't. I love you, darling, and now I know you love *me*, nothing else matters.'

He raised his head, his eyes glowing like dark coals. 'And you'll marry me?'

'Just try stopping me!'

Wordlessly his mouth gentled hers, his tongue delicately tracing her lips as his hands lightly moved over her body, as if trying to rediscover her.

'I can't believe we're together like this,' he said unsteadily.

'We could have been together earlier if you hadn't stayed away so long. It's been three months.'

'Until a few weeks ago I was convinced I meant nothing to you. In fact I kept expecting Gordon to tell me he was marrying you. Then, when he didn't, I began to think I'd misjudged the situation. That's when I decided to come and see you again. But I was scared you'd refuse to see me if I just turned up on your doorstep, so I concocted the idea of having you stay here for the weekend. The Marshalls were only too pleased to co-operate.'

'I thought the champagne and caviare a somewhat extravagant touch for them to lay on,' she chuckled.

'Nothing's too extravagant for you, my lovely Di. That's what's great about having money. Now I can give you everything you want.'

'All I want is you. It was all I *ever* wanted.'

'I know that now.'

Suddenly the humour was gone, replaced by a burning need to assuage the misery of the past months, the loss of the past years. Wordlessly Adam wrapped his arms around her, his warmth enveloping every fibre of her being as he stroked her hair and pressed kisses on her temple and cheek before finally finding her mouth. Deeply she breathed in the scent of him, her body trembling as the sweetness of it filled her lungs.

Murmuring deep in his throat, his arms came under her legs and lifted her up to cradle her against him. 'Any objections if we let the champagne go flat?' he whispered as he carried her out of the door and across the hall to the stairs.

'I'd object if we didn't!'

'We might even miss dinner.'

'I'm sure you'll fill me with something to replace it.'

'Again and again, my dearest heart. Again and again.'

Take 4 bestselling love stories FREE

Plus get a FREE surprise gift!

Fifty red-blooded, white-hot, true-blue hunks from every State in the Union!

Beginning in May, look for MEN MADE IN AMERICA! Written by some of our most popular authors, these stories feature fifty of the strongest, sexiest men, each from a different state in the union!

Two titles available every other month at your favorite retail outlet.

In September, look for:

DECEPTIONS by Annette Broadrick (California)
STORMWALKER by Dallas Schulze (Colorado)

In November, look for:

STRAIGHT FROM THE HEART by Barbara Delinsky (Connecticut)
AUTHOR'S CHOICE by Elizabeth August (Delaware)

You won't be able to resist MEN MADE IN AMERICA!

Calloway Corners

In September, Harlequin is proud to bring readers four involving, romantic stories about the Calloway sisters, set in Calloway Corners, Louisiana. Written by four of Harlequin's most popular and award-winning authors, you'll be enchanted by these sisters and the men they love!

MARIAH by Sandra Canfield
JO by Tracy Hughes
TESS by Katherine Burton
EDEN by Penny Richards

As an added bonus, you can enter a sweepstakes contest to win a trip to Calloway Corners, and meet all four authors. Watch for details in all Calloway Corners books in September.